OOPS!

———————

ALEXANDRA WARREN

SYNOPSIS

"As if sleeping with the enemy wasn't disastrous enough…"

For Camryn Cox, living a private, purpose-driven, drama-free life is a top priority. And in her opinion, Maverick Woods represents everything opposite of that.

He's social media-famous, ultra fine, and completely irresponsible, making him something like the enemy as far as Camryn is concerned. But everything changes when a surprise moment of passion between the two of them results in a positive pregnancy test.
Oops!

CAMRYN

I was going to kill Maverick Woods.

He had one job. One single, simple job that didn't even require him to leave his house to complete. But here we were, scrambling to find a replacement performer for this weekend's fundraising gala all because he'd foolishly decided to break up with the girl who was supposed to be donating her talent to the cause.

The girl we'd already spent thousands of dollars advertising.

The girl people had paid good money, *in the name of philanthropy*, to see.

And the girl who had now backed out because who would want to perform at a gala benefiting the foundation named after their ex's mother?

Really, the only thing I could blame her for was getting involved with Maverick in the first place. He was, *for lack of a better term*, a fuckboy from top to bottom.

The seasick waves, the thick, moisturized beard, the perfect white teeth that he sometimes liked to cover with a bottom row of golds...

The tattoos, the designer clothes and gaudy jewelry, the ridiculously priced sneakers...

Top to bottom wasn't an exaggeration by any means. And when you paired that with his knack for being a self-centered asshole, it made it hard for me to understand his appeal; especially for someone like Lillian Banks who was known for being one of the sweethearts of the Hollywood scene before she started showing up in pictures with Maverick.

Just like that, her whole image was exposed, going from the sweet songbird on every young adult sitcom to the party animal who was constantly getting caught by paparazzi after one too many. I mean, for her to have already been as big of a star as she was, it was wild to see how hooking up with the son of Meredith Woods put a totally different spotlight on her. But leave it to Maverick to ruin someone's entire reputation and then break up with them like it's nothing.

To him, it probably wasn't. But to us, the people making phone calls to everyone we knew trying to find someone to replace Lillian in this weekend's performance, it was the kind of stuff that made you want to choke the person on sight and deal with the consequences later.

Obviously, I couldn't do that if I wanted to keep my job. But with every negative response the foundation received thanks to the booking being so last minute, I considered it more and more, my shoulders tense as I dialed up another manager and started praying silently until they picked up.

"Caleb Peterson speaking."

Putting on my professional voice, I crooned, "Mr. Peterson, hi. This is Camryn Cox with the Meredith Woods Foundation. How are you?"

"I'm alright, and yourself?"

Releasing a heavy sigh, I answered honestly, "Well, I'll

be better if you have someone on your roster of talent that we could borrow for a gala we're hosting this weekend."

Like everyone I'd called before him, there was already some apprehension in his tone when he repeated, "This weekend? *Umm...*"

"I know it's super short notice. But unfortunately, our performer dropped out earlier this morning, and now we're desperate."

I was hoping the d-word would gain me some sympathy points, especially since it was the God-honest truth. But for Caleb, this was business, which meant his follow-up question was, "How much does the gig pay?"

"About that..." I started, getting ready to throw some words together that told this man the gig wasn't exactly a paying one in the most roundabout way possible. But it was almost like he could already sense that energy the way he interjected, "Ms. Cox, can I put you on a quick hold?"

"Sure," I answered sharply, fully expecting the hold to turn into him just hanging up on me. In fact, I was already scribbling his name off the list of calls we could make when my boss, Janet, popped in to ask, "Any luck?"

Like I didn't already know what the outcome of this call would be - *the same outcome of all twelve calls before it* - I covered the speaker with my hand so that I could whisper, "I'm on hold with Caleb Peterson right now."

Giving a nod, she popped back out just as quickly as she'd popped in. And thankfully so since that meant she didn't have to witness the disappointed look on my face when Caleb finally returned to the line just to say, "Ms. Cox, I apologize for the wait. But unfortunately, all of my artists are booked for the weekend."

"Of course they are," I thought to myself with a roll of my eyes, being polite about it when I replied, "I understand.

Thank you for your time." But once I hung up, I let out the most annoyed grunt, beyond frustrated with this entire ordeal just as the person responsible casually strolled into the building.

Janet greeted him warmly, and our receptionist did the same. But I couldn't get up and shut my office door fast enough. Though, of course, that was the thing that got his attention and sent him my way.

Annoying.

Through the one-way glass, I could see when he was getting closer. And once he stepped inside without invitation, I didn't even bother giving him my eyes, completely focused on the short list of names I had left to call when I asked, "Why are you here?"

"I was just coming in to see if y'all found somebody to replace Lillian at the gala this weekend. I can make a few phone calls if I need to."

Just the sound of his voice had me on edge, a scowl on my face as I peeked up to tell him, "Definitely should've done that before you decided to break up with the girl. But, sure. Make the calls, Mav."

For whatever reason, that made him smirk as he pulled out his phone to do so while I went back to my list. And even though I should've been making another call of my own just in case whatever he was doing fell through, I couldn't help eavesdropping on his conversation with the same person who'd just turned me down.

"*C.P. What's good, bruh?... Aye, I'm kinda in a bind with mom's foundation and need a favor... Oh, you just got off the phone with Camryn? Yeah, she's in charge of this whole thing... Mmhm... Mmhm... Yeah, that'll work... Bet. Appreciate you, man.*"

Admittedly, I was torn between being annoyed with Caleb for lying about his artists' availability and being annoyed with Maverick for existing once he ended the call and shared, "Aight, we got Constella."

"Constella?" I repeated with a frown, only vaguely remembering the name from my parents' music collection as Maverick explained, "Yeah, old school R&B. The people will love it."

Considering the age range of our biggest donors, I started to imagine a world where he was actually right. But when I could only think of maybe one or two songs by her, the annoyance settled right back in, my frown remaining when I asked, "Does she really have the range for something like this, though? I mean, can she still even sing?"

Like I'd asked a stupid question, Maverick groaned, "Yes, Camryn. Why else would Caleb have signed her?"

Once again, I wanted to believe him, wanted to release the stress-filled breath I'd been holding since this morning when Lillian's people first reached out to let us know she'd no longer be able to perform. But the truth was, "This is a disaster."

Dropping my head onto my desk, I felt Maverick's hand against my shoulder as he insisted, "Come on, Cam. Be optimistic."

"*Optimistic?*" I repeated, peeking up to remind him, "It's two days before the gala and we're replacing our money-making, popular performer with a... has been. All because you couldn't wait a couple days before ending things with Lillian."

Honestly, I still couldn't believe he'd done something so selfish, couldn't believe he'd put his mother's foundation and the gala in such an awful predicament without warning. And I was just about to go off on him about it until he quietly explained, "Camryn, Lillian was just admitted to a rehab facility a little bit ago. She wasn't performing this weekend regardless."

Oh.

Shit.

There was no use in hiding my shock when I repeated, "*A rehab facility?* You broke up with her, and the girl went straight to rehab?!"

Obviously, something like that couldn't have been completely his fault. But the timing of it still had me skeptical as Maverick scrubbed the back of his head before somberly answering, "Lillian had some demons she was dealing with. Shit got out of control, and *I*... there was just nothin' more I could do for her. I guess the breakup was the sign she needed to get some professional help."

Admittedly, the news made me a little sad since Lillian and I were close enough in age for me to feel like I could've been in the same predicament had life taken me down the path of stardom. But instead, I was stardom-adjacent, working for the last year as Director of Development and Fundraising for the charity foundation created by one of the most recognizable faces in black cinema, Meredith Woods.

As an actress, she wasn't nearly as active as she used to be by choice. But every once in a while, she'd pop up on a show or in a movie playing someone's hilarious mother or the stylish aunt. Basically characters that represented who she was in real life; an "auntie" to many and a mother to Maverick and his twin sister Malinda.

Malinda was just like her mother, making her easy to get along with.

But that brother of hers...

Rolling my eyes, I finally replied, "Well that's good for her, I suppose."

For whatever reason, that made Mav snicker. "Not a single empathetic bone in your body, huh?"

"I said good for her," I emphasized, shaking my head as I continued, "Still not good for us. I mean, no disrespect to this woman. But this is equivalent to paying for a ticket to see Ariana Grande perform, then getting to the show and it's actually Michel'le."

"Who has some bops," Maverick insisted. ""Something in My Heart"? "Nicety"? Come on now."

The fact that he knew Michel'le's greatest hits off the top of his head made it hard not to grin as I noted, "Sometimes Meredith being your mother makes absolutely no sense. And other times, *like now*, I can tell you really were raised by her."

Like he was proud of that fact, *which he should've been because Meredith was an amazing human*, he grinned back before asking, "So we're good? You got an artist, everything else is still a go…"

"Yep. All problems are solved thanks to your one phone call. *Whew.* What a lifesaver. How could we ever repay you?" I asked sarcastically, rolling my eyes again as he raised his phone to snap a pic of us together for "repayment".

"Say cheese, Cam," he sang, my face remaining completely stale in response as I flipped him the bird just as he tapped the screen to take the picture. "Camryn, I can't post this on my IG."

"That's the point," I groaned, scribbling down a note to create new gala promo announcing the artist change as Maverick decided, "*Actually…* I'll just crop you out."

"Even better," I told him, tossing my hand dismissively as I continued, "Now get. Some of us have real work to do."

"Hold on. I'm gonna do a little promo video real quick. Get people hyped about Constella and all that."

As a concept, it was a good idea, similar enough to the same thought I'd just had until I remembered, "Maverick, your girlfriend… *or*, ex-girlfriend, was just admitted to rehab. Do you really think you should be posting anything on social media right now? I mean, even if it hasn't become public information yet, they're still gonna link everything back to what you were doing when it does. And if you're out here looking all happy and normal while she's…" I trailed, not even needing to fill in the blank to be able to advise, "You should probably be laying as low as possible."

With the way these bloggers worked nowadays, I honestly wouldn't have been surprised if they'd already clocked Maverick coming here to the foundation instead of being with Lillian whenever she was admitted. But instead of worrying myself with something that was truly none of my business, I started to go back to my work until Maverick responded, "Sometimes, my mother hiring you to assist in running her foundation makes no sense. And other times, like now, I totally understand it."

Even with him phrasing his commentary to match mine, the backhandedness of his compliment still had my eyes tight as I threatened, "Please leave before I strangle you."

"*Damn.* Violence ain't gotta always be the answer, mamas," he laughed, making his way to the door before turning back to add, "And besides, if your hands are ever wrapped around my neck, it damn sure ain't gonna be cause you're tryna hurt me."

It was out of pure reflex when I grabbed the closest thing within arm's reach and launched it at him, a little bit tickled to watch Maverick dodge the item before he snapped, "Cam, what the fuck?! Were those scissors?"

I shrugged, smirking mischievously as I told him, "Had

to make sure my violence didn't get mistaken for anything else."

"What if they would've stabbed me? Or hell, poked my damn eye out?" he whined. "I could've been patch-bound like Slick Rick for the gala fuckin' around with you."

The thought alone made me cackle, even more so when I realized, "Considering this old ass artist you booked for us, it would've been very on-brand."

Chuckling a bit himself, Maverick stepped back inside of my office and insisted, "You hatin' now, but I bet you dinner she's gonna kill it."

My eyebrow piqued at his wager. "As in, I'll *UberEats* you a meal of choice if you're right and vice versa? Cause dinner with you, even with you treating, is still not exactly a win."

"It's a lotta women out here who would pay good money to have dinner with me, Camryn," he immediately defended. And while I couldn't exactly disagree, I also knew where I stood about it, laughing to myself as I rose from behind my desk and replied, "Oh, I'm well aware. And something is truly wrong with every last one of them."

Instead of responding right away, he took a second to ogle my full look of the day, an outfit I was too stressed to put much time into this morning after waking up to the news of our performer needing to be replaced. But considering the way Maverick slowly scraped his teeth against his bottom lip while sizing me up, you would've thought I had on nothing at all. And I was mad at myself for warming up a little in response to his gaze as he finally agreed, "Fine. *UberEats* then since you can't even stand to break bread wit' a nigga."

Again, I laughed. "Oh my God, why are you acting so butthurt? I mean, do you really think I wanna be the first girl you're seen out with after your breakup, even platonically? You tryna have the Banksy Boos coming after me too?"

"They ain't even that bad," he insisted with a shrug like Lillian's fan club hadn't been harassing his ass all over social media since the breakup and like he hadn't already done something in an attempt to contain some of the harassment.

I had that to lean on when I pointed to the phone in his hand while replying, "Open your newly-private *Instagram* and tell me that lie again."

"Aight, so maybe they are wildin' a little bit," he admitted. "But I didn't say dinner had to be at a public place."

"I know. It'll be in the privacy of my apartment where I'll devour fifty dollars' worth of some good eats on your dime while binging old episodes of The Bernie Mac Show, *alone.*"

The way he frowned in response, I assumed he was offended by my desire to exclude him from my plans. But to my surprise, it was... "*Fifty dollars?* I mean, I know those little convenience fees and shit add up, but damn."

"All that ballin' you do for the 'gram and you're trippin' over fifty bucks?" I asked amusedly, crossing my arms over my chest as he answered, "Nah, but you might be when you're wrong and gotta spend that same amount on me. I know my mama pays you well, *but...*"

Before he could finish, I cut him off with a gentle shove towards the door. "I'll see you Saturday at the gala, Maverick."

"Looking forward to it, Camryn," he replied with a wink that had my dimples threatening to make an appearance until I saw my boss lurking nearby, sending me on a not at all obvious dash back to my desk as Maverick told her, "Let me know if y'all need anything else, Auntie J."

With a kiss to her cheek, he disappeared to wherever as she curled into my office. And while I tried my best to make it look like I was working, I assumed Janet was getting ready to call my bluff once she started, "Patiently waiting on the day you two stop playing and get together already."

Wait a minute... huh?

My face went tight with confusion when I asked, "What two? Me and Maverick?"

Her enthusiastic nod in response made me snort a laugh that turned into much more as I told her, "Oh, Janet. I'm so sorry, but you'll have to ship us in your dreams cause there is no way in hell I'd ever date that man."

Like I was being ridiculous, she frowned while asking, "Why not? My nephew is cute!"

This time, it was me nodding as I continued to giggle and agreed, "He *is* cute. Very cute, and equally annoying."

"He's only like that cause he likes you," Janet reasoned with a grin, though her explanation really only gave more fuel to my giggles.

"What is this? Kindergarten? And why are you so convinced that Maverick likes me as if he wasn't just in a very serious relationship with someone else a literal two days ago?"

Brushing that off as nothing, Janet insisted, "Lillian was cool and all, but she's no you."

Truthfully, I wasn't in the business of comparison and had no shortage of confidence. But her statement made it way too easy for me to counter, "Tell the rest of America that, and they'll laugh right in your face the same way I've been doing."

That brought her frown back as I continued, "All of this is irrelevant anyway cause I don't even like Maverick like that."

I was stating it as a fact. But for whatever reason, Janet seemed just as sure when she replied, "Camryn, please. The only reason that boy gets under your skin the way he does is because you're trying so hard *not* to like him."

Her assumption felt like a Michael Jordan dunking in *Space Jam* kind of reach. I tolerated Maverick out of respect for his mother, respect for his family. We could share a room without me attacking him... *for five minutes at a time*. And maybe when I first started working for the foundation and just so happened to be in off-mode with my on-again, off-again boyfriend, I might've had an insta-crush since Maverick was the type of fine you only saw on the internet. But all of that stopped once I got to know him and his online persona that was so perfectly disappointing I couldn't help but laugh as I told Janet, "Trust me, I don't have to try at all. He makes himself very easy not to like."

"So what was all that flirting I just walked in on then?" she challenged, grinning as she crossed her arms in a stance that told me she thought she knew more than she did. But I was happy to bust her bubble, serving an equally sweet smile when I suggested, "A figment of your imagination, perhaps?"

My response made her eyes slip to more of a squint. "You really think you're slick, don't you?"

I didn't answer her question, choosing to pose one of my own instead. "Is there something work-related I can help you with? Cause I know we don't technically have an HR department around here, but I'm about ready to report you to your big sister for meddling."

"Meredith isn't going to do anything to me," she chuckled. "And really, you better hope she doesn't get wind of this cause she'll hassle you way more than I ever could."

"Good thing there's nothing for her to get wind of then,

huh?" I questioned with a smirk, doubling down on my claims in hopes that it would actually stick this time.

Thankfully, Janet didn't continue trying to convince me otherwise, instead nodding as she acknowledged, "Quick on your feet. I respect it."

"On the long list of reasons why you guys hired me," I reminded her, catching a bit of a side-eye that had me asking, "Too much?"

"Entirely," she answered. And I was just getting ready to apologize until she continued, "But I'll let it slide since I know that visit from your little boo still has you juiced up."

"*Oh my God*," I sighed as Janet giggled her way out of my office. And while her leaving should've been my cue to get back to work, I was too distracted with thoughts of everything she'd shared, leading me down the dark path to Maverick's *Instagram* where I discovered he'd completely disregarded my advice about laying low.

"A fuckin' car selfie? Seriously, Mav?" I groaned as I read the caption.

"Sun was hittin', so you know I had to do it to 'em one time."

There was no denying how fine he looked in the picture with his skin and beard glistening perfectly in the sunlight and his jewelry shining even brighter than it had in person.

But the timing…

Shaking my head, I went to the comments and saw people giving the same energy I'd warned him about earlier.

"Did you take this right after dropping Lillian off at rehab?"

"Taking selfies while Lillian is fighting for her life? What a dick."

"Lillian deserves so much better."

Knowing Maverick in real life, I was honestly more annoyed *for* him than I was *at* him since the slander was a bit overdone. I mean, these were the same people who were completely up his ass just last week. And now they all hated him because he'd made a personal decision?

The shit was truly ridiculous. But it was also the perfect reminder for me to not give any more thought to what Janet had shared.

Whether Maverick was into me or not didn't even matter. Cause regardless of how he felt, there was no way in hell I was putting myself in position to join his circus of drama and the scrutiny that came with it.

MAVERICK

"*Whew*. I made some beautiful ass children."

Grinning from ear to ear, I kept my arm wrapped around my sister's shoulder as we smiled for what had to have already been the thousandth picture of the night. But I'd take a thousand more if it meant keeping a smile on my mother's face as we held our pose for a few more snaps before continuing down the red carpet where there were a variety of reporters waiting to throw us questions about tonight's gala.

Because of the circumstances, I tried my best to hang in the back while my mother and sister did most of the talking. But it was inevitable that someone would try it by directly asking me, "Maverick, how are you feeling after the breakup? Do you believe it in any way contributed to Lillian's rehab admittance?"

Plastering on an empathetic smile, I answered, "I'm just glad she's getting the help she needs, and I wish her all the best. But tonight isn't about us. It's about the hundreds of youth who will benefit from the funds raised thanks to the interest of this amazing woman."

My mother shot me a bashful smile in response to the compliment before excusing us to the next group of media that were a little friendlier than the last and included some of the black publications my mother was always intentional in showing love to. Then we made our way to the end of the carpet where Camryn was supposed to be waiting to escort us inside.

Correction, where Camryn *was* waiting to escort us inside, looking so unrecognizably delicious that I had to do a double take.

Don't get me wrong, Camryn was pretty as hell on any given day. But tonight, her shit was just elevated in a way that intrigued me; every inch of her mocha brown skin glistening against the red gown that sat off her shoulders and her full lips perfectly tinted the same shade as she smiled at my mother before pulling her into a hug.

"Ms. Woods, you look amazing," she complimented, showing the same love to Malinda and giving me a short nod of acknowledgment as my mother replied, "As do you, Miss. Cox. I am living for this dress, honey."

"And I wanna get her out of it," was the salacious thought that flashed through my head as Camryn shared, *"Rent The Runway* saved your girl yet again," striking a little pose to go with it before giving us some instructions. "Okay, so what I'm gonna have you do, Ms. Woods, is link arms with Mav. Malinda, you'll take his other arm, and he'll escort you both to the stage for you to give a few opening remarks before we serve dinner."

My mother nodded as Camryn went on to say, "Malinda and Maverick, I know this isn't new to you, but I'll have you guys stand a few steps back for spotlight purposes. And *then...* what is it, Mav?"

I hadn't even realized I was staring so hard until

Camryn called me out on it. But it was hard not to with her looking so damn good, the jet-black bundles sitting against her clavicle just begging me to move them out of the way and replace them with my mouth as I cleared my throat to say, "Oh, nothin'. My bad. What were you saying?"

"Few steps back so we don't get in mama's light," Malinda answered for her before asking, "Anything else we need to know, Camryn?"

Glancing at the notes on her phone, she said, "Well originally, Maverick was going to introduce our performer for obvious reasons. But now that that's all changed..."

Before she could even start running alternate scenarios in her head, I interjected, "I can still do it."

"Are you sure?" Camryn asked, still looking a bit uncertain about the whole thing. But I was happy to put her at ease when I nodded and answered, "Positive. Don't even worry about it."

That seemed to bring her a little relief as she released a sigh that dropped her bare shoulders a notch. "Okay then, I think that's all. Enjoy tonight, and I'll be sure to take care of the rest."

"Thank you, Camryn. You're a gem," my mother sang, Cam giving a smile in return before leading the way towards our entrance while I stayed a few steps back and quietly agreed, "That she is."

"Don't you start, Maverick," Malinda whispered, nudging me in the arm as I instinctively played dumb.

"*What?* What I do?"

"I saw the way you were looking at her, bro," Malinda stated plainly, leaving no room for me to tell a story.

So I didn't, instead giving a little shrug when I asked, "I can't enjoy the view?"

"Mav, you have enough shit going on right now. The last

thing you need to be doing is enjoying any view," she scolded. And rightfully so since... *damn*, had the past week been trash.

The nasty breakup with Lillian.

Her fans coming for my neck in every way possible without knowing any details.

Her admittance to rehab that I was somehow getting blamed for, and the gala she'd dropped out of because of said admittance...

Long story short, my life had been a whirlwind. But I was trying to put all that shit in the back of my head so I could be present for tonight's event that was not only important to my mother and all the kids she served through her foundation, but also to Camryn who'd spent the last several months putting it all together.

It was her first big project since my mother and aunt hired her on about a year ago, a project I was supposed to be assisting on the same way I chipped in on all the foundation's initiatives. But Camryn was so damn competent that my assistance was really just getting in her way. And since there were plenty of other ways for me to spend my time, I fell back, letting her do her thing and admiring her work ethic from a distance while also being sure to take care of the one way I could easily contribute by having Lillian perform.

Obviously, I'd fucked that up. But in my heart, I knew Constella would be just as good if not better; especially since Lillian performing in her current condition would've been career suicide.

Even if we weren't together anymore, I still couldn't let her go out like that. I also couldn't ruin my mother's event - *Camryn's event* - by letting all the talk become about Lillian's performance instead of the youth she was raising money for.

So I did what I had to do, let Camryn chew me out

about it, and was now enjoying the sight of her from behind as she waited for the cue to send us out on stage.

Gotdamn, she was looking beautiful tonight.

I was trying to put my finger on exactly what it was about her. But really, it was everything.

All of it.

All of *her.*

The dress, the hair, the makeup, the body.

She was fuckin' stunning, and I wasn't ashamed to admit that I couldn't stop staring, not even when she peeked back to give us the cue to go.

My mother and sister moving prompted me to do the same while my eyes remained on Camryn's as she gave me a confused look like she didn't know how damn fine she was. But considering the night was only just beginning, I figured I had plenty of time to tell her about herself later, doing my best to focus on my job of getting my mother and sister to the stage without tripping over their dresses and smiling for all the footage being taken while my mother gave her remarks.

She kept it short and sweet, thanking everyone for attending, encouraging people to use the donation envelopes that were stationed near the centerpieces at each table, and finally telling them to enjoy their dinner along with the special guest performance and auction that would follow. Then just as quickly as I'd escorted them out, I was helping my mother and sister down the front stairs to our table where Aunt Janet and her husband Brett were already sitting.

"Looking good, family," Brett complimented as I pulled a chair for my mother and then Malinda. But once I sat down myself, I realized there was an extra seat next to mine, causing me to feel hopeful for all the wrong reasons until

Aunt Janet shared, "That one was supposed to be for Lillian."

"Oh. *Right*," I sighed, grateful that our server was coming around to fill our champagne flutes since it was clear I'd need to be under some sort of influence to get through the night. And by the time dinner was finished, I was feeling nice, just tipsy enough for the words to flow freely once I saw Camryn gesturing for me to join her side stage in preparation for Constella's introduction.

"Showtime, folks," I announced to my table with a grin before excusing myself, stopping to say what's up to a few familiar faces on my way to where Camryn was waiting. But now that we were finally alone, *and she was still looking just as good as she had before my meal,* Constella was the last person on my mind, my full attention on Camryn as I told her, "I really wanna gas you right now, but I'm afraid you might try to hurt me."

"Hurt you over a compliment when I need you looking good out there in exactly three minutes? I would never," she insisted, glancing at the time on her phone as I decided to come straight out with what was on my mind.

"Aight, so let me just say this then. If you weren't you, I'd probably be tryna smash."

Admittedly, that wasn't the full truth since her being her really wasn't stopping anything. I suppose I just called myself trying to, *at least*, be a little polite about it; though it wasn't enough to keep Camryn from frowning when she asked, "That's a compliment? Cause I'm pretty sure you'd also smash a pepperoni *Hot Pocket* if it was microwaved just right."

The specificity of her response made me bust out laughing. "Aye, you funny for that. But I'm for real, though. You look amazing tonight, Cam. Almost too damn good," I told her with a slow onceover that had her dimples showing as she rushed out, "Well you also look great tonight, so there's that."

"*Whaaat?* Camryn Cox is actually being nice to me?" I asked teasingly, moving a little closer to whisper in her ear, "Shit, a nigga might just have to press his luck then. What's up?"

I was really only messing around, but the giggle she responded with told me I might not have been as far off as I thought even when she pushed me away while squealing, "Maverick, get your ass out on that stage."

Straightening out my suit jacket, I did just that, making my way to the mic and then waiting until the room settled a bit before I started, "How's everyone doing tonight? For those of you who don't know me, I'm Maverick Woods, completely blessed to be the only son of actress, philanthropist, and best mama on the planet, Meredith Woods."

There was a hoot from the back of the room that encouraged me to add, "Yeah, give it up for her, y'all."

The room exploded in applause that had my mother beaming with gratitude as she shot me a wink while I continued, "Now before I introduce our special guest, I wanted to take a moment to say thank you to everyone who has already contributed to the cause and everyone who plans to contribute before the night is over. The work done by the foundation wouldn't be possible without your support. And these kids, man. They deserve it."

"I'd also like to give a special shoutout to the person who's responsible for putting all of this together, our director of development and fundraising, Miss. Camryn Cox."

When I peeked over to side stage, I could tell the acknowledgment had caught her off-guard. But knowing all the work she'd put in to make this happen, it was only right to let my genuine appreciation be known publicly, my eyes remaining her way as I spoke, "Camryn, these people wouldn't have the opportunity to give us their money if it wasn't for you, so thank you."

The crowd gave a murmur of a laugh at that even though I was deadass, but it served as the perfect transition for me to get to what I was really on stage for when I finished, "Now, without further ado, I need y'all to make a lot of noise for the woman who was not only so gracious in lending her talents to the cause at the last minute, but will also be blessing us with her first live performance in over two decades... Constella!"

There was another round of applause as the spotlight dropped and the curtain behind me began to open while I returned to side stage, the fact that the crowd already seemed hyped making it easy for me to brag, "That fifty dollars' worth of *UberEats* is gonna *slap* when this shit is over with."

"Fuck off, Mav," Camryn groaned playfully just as Constella's band started vibing. And once she hit the stage, there was an obvious appreciation for our replacement performer, the donors going up the second she acknowledged them with a raspy, "*How's everyone feelin' tonight?*"

She continued on with some spiel about being excited to be here, grateful for the opportunity and all that. But my attention mostly remained on Camryn as I reminded her, "That's how you wanted it, right? I mean, I'd be happy to share twenty bucks worth of Fatburger, *but...*"

"Fine," she conceded. "Text me your order. I'll pick it up on my way back to the office since I have a bunch of stuff I need to drop off when this is over anyway. You can meet me there."

With a nod, I agreed to her plan just as Constella really

started killing it on the stage, even inviting my mother up to do one of her signature dance routines from back in the day. But it was honestly the most fun I'd ever seen people have at one of these things, so I was grateful everything had worked out the way it did, grateful that Camryn had given me a chance to make it right.

She was vibing in her own little world as Constella went into her final song of the night, the hit love ballad everyone knew her by, *"Galaxy Love"*.

Just like the rest of the audience, Camryn mouthed along to the words as Constella belted the song with a little more maturity in her voice than when it was first recorded decades ago. The shit still sounded fire, though. And with the mood it was creating, I couldn't help pulling Camryn in for a little dance, surprised when she didn't fight me off after I tossed my arm around her from behind and started swaying to the beat.

Don't get me wrong, she wasn't completely committed. But she wasn't exactly trying to get rid of me either, just letting me have my moment until Constella hit her final note and the crowd erupted in applause.

As the curtains closed, a promotional video began to play that chronicled all the work the foundation had done over the past year, mostly things I had shown up for for photo-op purposes while leaving the real work to the other volunteers and paid staff. But watching that same video bring tears to Camryn's eyes had me feeling a way; wanting to step my game up, wanting to do something that mattered, wanting to get more involved in ways only I could so that I could feel the same emotions she was feeling about it.

That's how the first donation happened.

The auction had just barely gotten started when I threw ten stacks at a damn five-day vacation in Cabo San Lucas that I could've easily gotten for a fraction of the price through my travel agent. But with the kids on my mind, and my sister taunting me with her equally competitive bids, I couldn't help myself, happy to accept my prize and see the smile on Camryn's face since my donation meant she was one step closer to her fundraising goal.

I still kept my bidding card to myself for the rest of the auction, though. But it didn't matter since between the auction items and the donor envelopes collected throughout the night, the foundation had easily surpassed its goal, the rest of the gala spent celebrating with more champagne to the sounds of Constella's band until the crowd began to fizzle out closer to midnight.

It was a good time, made even greater by the fact that I had a fatburger with cheese and some skinny fries waiting on me back at the office. But when I showed up to find Camryn scowling over her own skinny fries and a strawberry shake, I worried my high was about to be blown, hardly wanting to ask, "What's the matter wit' you?"

Peeking up like she hadn't even heard me come in, her scowl turned into more of a frown when she answered, "Just a little disappointed is all."

"*Disappointed?* Camryn, tonight was amazing. Everyone had a wonderful time, Constella killed it, the fundraising goal was exceeded…"

"Yes, the foundation's fundraising goal was exceeded. But my personal fundraising goal for tonight came up…" she paused, glancing at her paper to confirm, "Twenty-five hundred dollars short."

"Overachieving ass," I chuckled, pulling my phone from my pocket so that I could give my second donation of the night; three thousand dollars sent via *PayPal*. "You should be good now."

Because she didn't know exactly what I was up to, my sentiment confused her until her phone buzzed with a notification. And while the skepticism remained on her face, all that changed once she read the screen and popped up out of her seat with a shocked, "*Maverick...*"

"Just say thank you, Camryn," I insisted with a smirk, getting ready to reach for what I assumed was my food sitting on her desk until she moved to throw her arms around my neck in a hug.

"I... thank you. *Seriously.* You have no idea how much this means to me."

Having Camryn this close, smelling all good and still looking just as amazing as she did at the gala had me swallowing hard so that I could appropriately respond, "Anything for the kids, right?"

Her voice took a different tone when she dropped her arms to quietly agree, "Yeah. The kids."

"And you too," I added, pulling her back my way to expand, "I'd do anything for you too."

There was a moment of silence, *a switch*, a distinct change in the energy between us as Camryn stared me down like she was trying to make sense of what I'd just said. But as the one who'd uttered the words and meant that shit, I had no problem keeping that same energy when I cupped her chin and brought my face down to hers for what was supposed to only be a brush of a kiss that quickly turned into a whole lot more once I got hip to just how good her lips tasted.

In no time at all, my hands were all over her body, my dick rock hard as the heat of her pussy began to emanate right from the slit of her dress. And with her tongue exploring every inch of my mouth, it was hard to catch my breath, though I made sure to catch just enough to request,

"Say yes, Camryn."

The last thing I wanted was for her to act like this shit was all my doing when it was all said and done. And no matter how hard it would be, I was fully prepared to pull the reins back if I had to; though I would've been lying if I didn't admit how grateful I was when Camryn responded with a sensual grin and the only words I needed to hear.

"Yes, Maverick."

My dick twitched in response as I backed her into the edge of her desk, our lips reconnecting as I started to remove my suit jacket before letting Camryn take over since she had a better angle. And it was her assistance that encouraged me to give a little of my own - *mainly so I could get between her thighs quicker* - the fit of her gown giving us a bit of a problem, especially once she breathily reminded me, "Be careful. I still have to mail this back."

"Should've known this sexy ass dress was gonna be my demise," I chuckled, brushing kisses against her neck as I suggested, "Let me just get you out of it. All the way."

Honestly, I expected her to argue against that idea, expected her to be on some "good girl" shit and fearful of the possibility of being seen. But I was pleasantly surprised when she just turned around so that I could get the zipper, the sight of her in only her strapless bra and thong once she stepped out of her gown literally taking my breath away and making sense of why I hadn't been able to stop looking at her all night.

Camryn in the red gown was a showstopper, no question. But it was what was hiding underneath that really made that shit go, my mouth watering as I took her all in before acknowledging the obvious.

"You are so fuckin' fine."

"And yet, you still have your pants on. Why?" she challenged, cocking her head to the side with a smirk as I let off a little laugh before lifting her sexy ass on top of her desk and answering her question with action.

Not the action she expected of removing my pants, but action she clearly appreciated considering the way her head was tossed back once I dropped to my knees to taste her pussy. Of course, her lower lips were just as delicious as the ones on her face. But it was her enthusiastic moans that had me losing my damn mind, putting my whole face in it like this wasn't supposed to be a quick, in the moment fuck.

Nah, I was doing the most. But it felt like I couldn't help myself, quickly becoming an addict for the taste of her, the sounds she made, the way she cuffed the back of my head to guide me, and the way her thighs clenched to signal she was close.

"Please. I need it," she begged as encouragement for me to keep going, flickering my tongue against her clit until her pussy began to throb with an orgasm. But not even then did I let up, licking at every bit of her release before standing up to share a kiss with her flavor.

"Tell me what else you need, Camryn."

Like me, she answered my question with the action of undoing my belt and the button of my pants, keeping me close enough to kiss as she followed with the zipper. And without fully removing my briefs, she blindly aligned us, our tongues tied as I slowly entered her with a moan that had my toes curling in my damn shoes.

Yeah, her pussy was a problem. But I wasn't no bitch, so I did what I had to do, Camryn's legs wrapped around my waist as I gave her more inches than she claimed she could handle but still never backed down from taking which solidified new meaning for the "good girl" I always thought of her as.

She was being a good girl, alright, every file and folder on her desk shifting with each stroke. But none of that seemed as important to her as me being inside of her, her voice growing hoarse as she begged me not to stop until she came again with a full-body shudder that damn near had me seeing stars as I painted her walls with my seed.

"*Gotdamn*," I hissed as Camryn released her legs from around me, my chest heaving as I pulled out with a grunt while she pushed me in the same spot so that she could get down.

Her frantic change in energy made it less of a surprise when she said, "We shouldn't have done that." And while I probably should've been taking her more seriously, I could only laugh.

"Cam, you was just tellin' me how bad you needed it. And now we shouldn't have done it?" I asked, truly amused by her switch as she nodded while answering, "Yes. Exactly that. Now help me back into my dress, please."

Since she already had it pulled up and in position for me to zip, I figured it was the least I could do. Though I also couldn't help questioning, "So all that noise you were just making was a lie, or…?"

"No, it wasn't a lie, Mav," she admitted, her head low as she continued, "Your dick… *and mouth*… were great. Five stars. But we still shouldn't have done it."

Fixing my pants, I challenged, "Because it was wrong, or because it only made you wanna do it again?"

"Maybe both? *I don't know.* I just… you should probably get going," she rushed out, turning to grab the *Fatburger* bag from her desk and shoving it into my hands the second I was finished with my belt buckle. "Here. Take your food."

Her urgency only made me laugh again. "Camryn,

what's really the problem here? I mean, we're both grown, both fine. This shit was honestly inevitable."

Ever since Camryn had started working at the foundation, I knew it wasn't an "if" but a "when" situation. And honestly, how I'd kept my distance for this long was a miracle until she reminded me, "You just got out of a relationship, and I could say the same. I work for your family, *at this desk*, and…"

"And now when you're busy organizing more fundraising efforts for the youth, you'll also have the fond memories of what I just did to you. You're welcome," I finished for her with a smirk that had her rolling her eyes as I grabbed my suit jacket to leave. But not without her catching me by the arm for one last plea.

"Hey. Let's just… pretend like this didn't happen, okay?"

There was legit panic in her eyes that had me wondering what I'd missed. I mean, it wasn't like we'd done something that damn scandalous. At least, not to my standards.

Then again, maybe that was it. Maybe an experience like this was just so out of her norm that she didn't know how to handle the aftermath. But as for me, the one who'd enjoyed every single second of what had happened between us and had no regrets, there was no reason not to be completely honest when I replied, "You can pretend all you want to, Camryn. *But your pussy? I'll never forget.*"

CAMRYN

The regret was instant.

There was no post-sex glow, no moment of shared bliss, not even a smile the second I realized what had really happened between Maverick and me. And it wasn't just the actual act that had me shook, but also the fact that I'd given him permission to take it there in the first place.

Was I that damn desperate?

I wasn't. I knew that. But leave it to Maverick's ass to have me questioning myself, trying to make sense of whatever the fuck had just happened on my desk at his mother's foundation of all places.

In my office-working woman fantasies, it was a dream come true. But in real life, it was a nightmare that had me scrambling to put my desk back together as each part of the night played back in my head; starting with the gala.

From the second Maverick laid eyes on me - *or rather, we laid eyes on each other cause the man looked disgustingly good in a suit* - I should've known some nonsense was about to ensue. I mean, how was I not supposed to fall for his constant charm, his heated attention, his awful yet somehow still flattering compliments, his... *touch?*

He *touched* me; held me for a dance. And the shit was so comfortable that it honestly scared me stiff as I struggled - *and failed* - to come up with a reason to knock him away in the moment.

Of course, I could come up with a boatload now. But in comparison to the rest of the night, that part of it was honestly mild.

Being giddy about his big donation, *even for an auction item*, kept my guard non-existent. Inviting him back to the office for some late-night eats was completely my fault. And then being excited to the point of doing my own touching in response to his second donation and letting the high of it all lead me straight into a kiss with consent for more?

Yeah, I set myself up with that one. And now here I was, trying to piece it all back together as if Maverick would ever let me live this shit down.

"At least he made it sound sexy..." I thought as I pulled out my phone and saw he'd just recently shared something to his *Instagram* story, the sight sending me into a panic until I realized, "This motherfucker went straight to the strip club?"

On one hand, I was relieved that there was no mention of what had just occurred between us. But on the other hand, I *was...* a little offended.

I mean, here I was, trying to dissect every detail. Still entirely too affected to even move. And he'd just gone on with his life as normal like nothing had even happened.

Isn't that what you wanted, Camryn?

The thought made me release an annoyed grunt as I grabbed a handful of fries and shoved them in my mouth, spitting them right back out into my hand once I realized they were cold. And when I tried to wash the residual salt down with my strawberry shake, even that wasn't hittin' the same, a frown on my face as I added those to the list of ways Maverick had ruined my night.

Somehow, the ways he'd made it was still longer. But instead of dwelling on that knowing it was a dead-end, I jumped over to check out the hashtag we'd used for the event, seeing all of our happy patrons putting me in a better mood until a series of text messages popped up at the top of my screen.

"U up?" — Nate

"Come through." — Nate

"I miss you." — Nate

"*Oh, hell no...*" I groaned, glaring at the thread of texts from my ex who had to be drunk or something equivalent to think I'd respond to his request favorably. In fact, I started to cuss his ass out until I realized no response at all would be more impactful, clearing the message and jumping to a new thread to send out an S.O.S to my best friend, Andria.

"Please tell me you're awake right now…" - Camryn

Just as I finished tightening up my desk, a response came through.

"I opened one eye to read and respond to this text, and I can't guarantee it'll open again." - Andria

Knowing she didn't play about her sleep, I had no reason not to believe her. But I also knew if she got wind of what I had to share, it would be the equivalent of an espresso shot, taking my chances when I gave her a brief overview of the past hour.

"I fucked Maverick and I'm pretty sure Nate is drunk-texting me." - Camryn

"Girl! What?! Come over! I'll open some wine!" - Andria

"That's what I thought," I muttered with a bit of a chuckle as I locked up the office before heading her way, the silent drive helping my nerves settle a bit by the time I pulled up to her place.

Still, it wasn't enough to keep the smirk off of Andria's lips the second she greeted me with an oversized wine glass and realized, "Oh, that dick was *good*, wasn't it?"

Accepting the glass from her hand, I downed it in a few

easy gulps, wiping the excess with the back of my hand before I answered, "You have no idea."

"Well paint the picture, girl. Set the scene. Give me details," she urged, inviting me inside and taking my empty glass so that she could refill it while I plopped down on the couch and got straight into my recap.

"Okay, so after the gala..."

"How was that, by the way?" she interrupted, being a real friend by actually showing interest in my endeavors instead of only being present for the tea. And honestly, with how smoothly things had gone on that front, I couldn't help but crack a real smile when I answered, "It went well. Constella was amazing, everyone seemed to have a good time, and the foundation met its fundraising goal."

Handing me a fresh glass, she took a sip from her own before settling in the seat next to mine. "I'm so glad to hear that. Congrats, girl. Now proceed."

With a quick sip, I restarted, "Okay, so after the gala, Maverick met me back at the office because we had a little bet going on..."

Without letting me explain, Andria interjected, "You betted on your pussy? *Camryn Coachella Cox...*"

"No! Of course not," I whined. "And Coachella? Really?"

Shrugging, she insisted, "Until you tell me what the C stands for, I have no choice but to use my imagination."

"I've told you a thousand times, Andi. It's literally just a C. It doesn't stand for anything."

Growing up, I never understood why my parents hadn't gotten more creative, leaving it up to people like Andria to assume silly shit like, "Okay, Camryn Crucial Conflict Cox."

"*Anyway,*" I groaned. "The bet was about Constella's performance, how well she'd hold the crowd after all these years of being off the scene or whatever. It was supposed to be fifty bucks of *UberEats*, but he suggested *Fatburger*. And since I didn't even really get a chance to sit down and eat at the gala, I agreed to it."

"Fatburger and fuckin'? *Whew*, you are speaking my language," she sighed, damn near going into a daydream about it until she realized, "But, wait. How did y'all go from sharing a meal to sharing genitalia?"

"Well, after getting the final numbers on how much we raised at the gala, I realized that while we'd met the public goal, I was still a few thousand short of my personal goal. And once Mav found out, he sent the money right over."

"Ahh, so you were bustin' it wide open for charity? That checks out," she said with a sure nod and a sip from her glass that had me quick to defend, "It wasn't *just* for charity. But that in combination with what he said and how he was looking at me *just*… it made me weak."

Even now, I shivered a little bit when I thought about that moment, Andria putting it lightly when she insisted, "As a fellow fine mothafucka, we tend to have that effect on people."

"Andi, I'm being serious!" I whined.

"So am I!" she yelled back, the chuckles that followed making it pretty clear that she was telling a lie. "But, okay. So he gave you the look, and you got weak. That still doesn't exactly explain how you ended up on the man's dick."

Releasing a heavy sigh, I shared, "He kissed me. *Sweetly.* Like, almost lovingly. And you know I'm a sucker for some good ass kissing."

"I do," she agreed. "But I also know you can keep your clothes on doing that, so… how did we get to the dick again?"

"Shit got hot, and he asked," I stated plainly, mimicking his tone when I crooned, "*Say yes, Camryn.*"

"Oh, this mothafucka was on his Floetry shit? No wonder you let him hit," Andria concluded with another chuckle as I corrected, "Girl, hit is an understatement. That man got me out of my gown and *dined.*"

Admittedly, I was still a little shook by how enthusiastic Maverick was about eating me out. He'd always struck me as the type to make sex all about him and his needs. But in reality, it was the exact opposite, the thought of his face between my thighs making it hard not to grin when Andria said, "Should've known that lush ass beard came from somethin'. And I can assume that if the kissing was good, the head game *was...*"

"Sensational. Breathtaking. Tens across the board, baby," I cheered, the wine clearly starting to affect me considering the way Andria's eyes filled with amusement.

Or hell, maybe it was my own eyes going glossy.

Either way, I was in a good mood as Andria replied, "First of all, congratulations. Second of all, how are we still not at the dick?"

"*Good question,*" I thought, realizing just how caught up on the details I was when I finally continued, "So after he made me cum with his mouth, I was lowkey concerned the dick might not live up to the hype. Like, this shit *has* to be too good to be true. And it was *not.*"

"Ooh, what it look like?" Andria squealed. "Long and skinny? Short and girthy? Veiny? Smooth? He's kinda tall, so I'd put money on the first one."

"Honestly, I didn't even really look at it," I admitted. "We were making out, and I just put it in."

Thinking back on it now, it felt like a missed opportunity since it wasn't like I'd ever give myself a reason to see it again. But Andria saw my oversight a bit differently, sounding proud about it when she replied, "Damn, girl. You must've really been in the zone."

"I was," I agreed with a nod. "But once it was over, reality set in and I panicked."

"Panicked, how?"

"Pushed him away, kicked him out, begged him to act like it never happened," I listed, saying it out loud making me feel silly.

Andria only made that feeling double in size when she asked, "Camryn, why? I mean, what's the big deal? Y'all smashed. The shit was bomb. Now you flush the condom and get over it."

"*About that...*" I trailed, diverting my eyes as I took a big gulp from my wine glass to keep from having to explain myself.

Of course, Andria caught on anyway, leaning in closer to ask, "Camryn Constella Cox, please tell me you used protection."

"It was such a heat of the moment thing, *and...*"

"He pulled out?" she interrupted, her head cocked as she waited for an answer. But when I could only respond with a weak, "*Umm...*" that set her on fire, hopping up from the couch to squeal, "Wow! You let Maverick Woods nut in you in the office suite named after his mother? Might have to hang your jersey in the rafters for that legendary performance."

"It's not funny, Andi," I whined even though I could barely get the words out without laughing thanks to the wine coursing through me.

"Not funny to *you*," Andria insisted with a laugh of her own, falling back into her seat as she continued, "But seriously, I'm here for Camryn Cardi Cox being a little reckless for a change. You deserved a good dickin' down with a donation on top after how hard you've been working on that gala these last few months."

Putting it like that, I couldn't help but agree with her. "I can admit, it *was* very stress relieving. *Until it wasn't.*"

"Only because you made it that way," she insisted. "Just appreciate it for what it was and leave it at that. I'm sure Maverick is steps ahead of you in that regard."

"He's at the strip club," I blurted. "I saw it on his *Instagram* story."

I don't know why that fact still made me feel a way, but it did. And it wasn't even about his chosen destination, more so about how easily he'd bounced to the next thing like he hadn't just fucked me senseless; like his beard didn't still smell like my pussy.

"See what I mean," Andria commented, pulling me from my thoughts to say, "He's not trippin', and you shouldn't be either."

Nodding, I agreed, "You're right. I'm buggin'. It was just sex. *Words I've never had to say in my life...*"

Admittedly, that was part of why I was struggling to process it all. Engaging in casual relations was unchartered territory for me since I was used to having sex with whoever I was in a relationship with and that's it. And considering that had only been one person for the last three years, being so open for Maverick was... *wild*, to say the least.

"Welcome to the club, girlfriend. We have lube samples to the left and Plan Bs to the right," Andria teased. "Now what was that you said about Nate's triflin' ass?"

Hearing his name was enough to make my nose wrinkle, another sip from my wine glass necessary before I explained, "Girl, he just texted me asking me to come through because he misses me. Like, you're the one who suggested we take a break to see other people. And now that you've obviously hit a standstill, I'm supposed to just come running back into your arms?"

I expected Andria to gas me up and agree. But instead, she only groaned, "It wouldn't be the first time, Cam."

"And you know what that is? *Growth*," I insisted, finishing off my glass to celebrate my damn self as Andria asked, "Did you text him back?"

"Hell no. Fuck him," I snapped.

Though, for whatever reason, my response only made Andria laugh as she sang, "O-kay. New dick got you livin' large and takin' charge. I see you, boo."

"Nah, it's not about Maverick at all. I gotta stop playin' myself when Nate has made it clear, *several times*, that he's not tryna settle down. At least not with me," I sighed, mad that I'd already finished off my wine since a sip would've been perfect for swallowing down that tough reality.

It had been exactly four years since I met Nate through a mutual friend, three years since we'd officially started dating, and two months since we'd gone on our third "break".

What I thought was going to be a conversation about taking our relationship to the next level, whether that be marriage or simply moving in together, turned out to be a conversation about why we should test the waters to make sure we were ready. And while I didn't need to test the waters to know shit, I suppose it was my love for Nate that made me agree to it. Though it didn't take long for me to realize that he was only using it as a "get out of jail free card" to fuck other people, leaving me with a choice to make.

Do I stick around and tolerate his bullshit, or do I make this "break" permanent?

Unfortunately, the question was answered for me when Nate stopped responding to my calls and texts, signaling to me that shit between us was over and done with. But of course, now that I had fully moved on in my mind, he was hitting me up to come through, a frustrated frown on my face just from thinking about it all as Andria coached, "Don't you dare get in your feelings over that piece of shit. You gave him more than enough of your time and energy. Now it's off with that nigga's noggin. Figuratively speaking, of course. *Unless...*"

Before she could get any crazy ideas, I interjected, "Nah, we don't need anybody going to jail."

"You sure? Cause my cousin Hantrell said he doesn't mind it. Last time he was in, he got his GED *and* a *Facebook* page."

"Are those... the same?" I asked, my head cocked and my eyebrows furrowed at her phrasing that she shrugged off like nothing.

"I'm just sayin'. And you know he's had a little crush on you ever since I brought your bougie ass to the cookout that one time. I'm sure he'd be happy to knock Nate's face in for you if it meant he could take you on a date after he was done."

While the thought of someone knocking Nate's face in did bring me a spurt of joy, having to tolerate a date with one of Andria's crazy ass cousins to make it happen seemed like the exact kind of stress I needed to be avoiding right now. Still, I tried to be polite about it when I told her, "I think I'm gonna pass. But thank you, and Handrail."

"Hantrell, girl. Han-*trell,*" she corrected, making me think back on what I'd actually said just as my phone buzzed with a text.

Since I hadn't responded to Nate, I expected it to be

him. But when I glanced at the screen and saw who it actually was, I was torn between being intrigued and annoyed as I clicked to read the full message.

"Round two? This liquor got me feelin' nasty as fuck right now." - Maverick

Whoa.

Bringing the phone closer to my face, I read it again to make sure I wasn't trippin'. Then I showed it to Andria for a second opinion, her reaction letting me know I wasn't imagining things once she gasped, "*Bitch.* You are in danger."

"I don't even know what to say to this!" I yelled, growing hot all over to the point that even the phone began to feel warm in my hands.

Of course, Andria was amused about it all, her tone laced with tease when she asked, "Do you want a round two with Mavy Mav, or nah?"

"No. *Yes.* Shit, I don't know. I'm too inebriated to make a wise decision!"

"But not too inebriated to use words like… *inebriated,*" she replied with a side-eye that had me quick to defend, "Don't judge my vernacular."

Brushing me off, she put in her real two cents. "All I'm gonna say is… if I was you, and it was as good as you said it was the first time, I wouldn't be turning down the possibility of him being even nastier."

Points were definitely made, especially since, "I'm so disturbed by how wet that text made me."

"Shit, I'm wet too, and he wasn't even asking me,"

Andria whined before suggesting, "Let's tag team his fine ass."

Honestly, the thought of sharing Maverick with anyone made me want to fight. And considering how ridiculous that was after one little... *slip-up*, the only logical conclusion was, "I can't mess with him again. Not after making such a big deal about the first time."

With a wave of her hand, Andria insisted, "If you're throwin' ass, I'm sure he'll understand."

Again, valid points were made, forcing me to give Andria credit when I told her, "You're a bad influence."

"Just tryna help you live your best life, sis. Now what are you gonna respond?"

Glancing at my phone, I decided, "I'm not going to, because he's obviously drunk and I don't need those kinds of problems in my life." But it was almost like he'd heard me with how quickly my phone buzzed with a fresh text.

"Come on, mamas. Respond to a nigga. I needs that bad." - **Maverick**

After peeking over my shoulder to see what had me frozen, Andria suggested, "Camryn, I think we might need to bow our heads and pray cause making it through this is gonna take some serious discipline."

"Girl, who you tellin'?" I whined as Andria grabbed my free hand and started, "Dear God, please cover Camryn C. Cox during this trying time. If you were wondering, the C stands for Coochie."

My snort of a laugh only made me start laughing even harder when I asked, "Why do you play so much?"

"I just didn't want Him covering the wrong folks. Had to make sure He knew exactly who I was talking about," she insisted, only making me giggle more as I started to type out a reply. *"Wait.* Are you actually responding?" Her question should've snapped me out of it. But after his second, *desperate* text, I just couldn't help myself, pressing send before I could change my mind.

"**Need is a very strong word, Maverick."** - Camryn

"**I know. And I meant every letter, including the s. So what's your address?"** - Maverick

Biting my lip, I went back and forth on what to respond as Andria asked, *"So....* when he comes over here, you taking the beard and I'm taking the dick? Or you want the dick and I'll take the beard? I'm honestly not picky."

Even though I knew she was only joking, I still threw her a mean side-eye that had her raising her hands in defense as I decided to tell Mav the truth.

"**I'm actually not at home."** - Camryn

"**How soon can you be?"** - Maverick

"Girl, you better take your ass on," Andria urged, all but

ready to shove me off the couch towards the door until I pointed towards my twice-emptied wine glass sitting on the table. "*Ooh.* Good point. Dick can give you life, but going after dick shall not take it. Hoe Proverbs 6:9."

My giggles were hard to control as I finally typed out a response.

"Umm... I'm a little tipsy, so no time soon."
- Camryn

"Liquor got you feelin' as nasty as me? ;)"
- Maverick

"Yes, Daddy. I'm so wet," Andria groaned from over my shoulder in her best blonde pornstar voice, my stomach beginning to hurt from laughing so hard as she used her regular voice to add, "I'ma need you to step your flirting game up, though. *All these dry ass replies...*"

Instead of taking her advice only to end up sounding silly as hell in the process, I played it safe by sticking to what I knew - *simplicity*.

"Maybe." - Camryn

"I'll come get your fine ass right now if I have to." - Maverick

His determination made it hard not to grin, my dimples at maximum depth as I replied with an important reminder.

"Mav, you're drunk. You shouldn't be driving." - Camryn

"I won't. I'll take an Uber. Now tell me where I'm going." - Maverick

Like I didn't know her address, Andria immediately started rattling it off for me to copy down, my fingers following her lead until I pressed send along with a plea for his safety.

"Please be careful." - Camryn

"Getting to you? I will. But once I get you? I can't make any guarantees ;) ." - Maverick

"Damn, he's good at this," I thought to myself, struggling not to get too wrapped up in all the flattery as Andria asked, "Bitch, are y'all already in love? What the fuck is all this cutesy shit?"

The fact that she'd noticed too had me quick to try and play it off. "Girl, relax. I'm just living my best life like you wanted me to."

"I mean, yes," she agreed with a nod. "But we also don't love these hoes, Camryn. Don't get too attached."

"Yeah, Camryn. Don't get too attached," I repeated in my head, trying to convince both Andria and myself when I replied, "Trust me. This is just... a moment. Cause ninety-five percent of the time, Maverick is otherwise too annoying to tolerate. We'll be back to regularly-scheduled programming come Monday."

It sounded good coming off my lips. But when I woke up a few hours later, *notably with my gown still intact,* I realized it wouldn't even take until Monday since I'd never actually made it off of Andria's couch.

"Wait. What happened?" I thought, my head pounding as I started to wonder if I'd only drunkenly dreamed up the entire thing. And when I picked up my phone and saw no notifications, I assumed it really must've been my nighttime imagination until Andria appeared out of nowhere to say, "That mothafucka has a lot of nerve doing all that beggin' just to stand you up."

Squinting my eyes against the sunlight coming through her living room window, I asked, "So all of that really did happen?"

"Yes, Camryn. Were you that drunk?" she questioned, passing me a bottle of *Pedialyte* that told me she already knew the answer since she was offering a remedy for my hangover.

Still, the more I tried to remember exactly how I'd gotten to this point, the more my head started to pound, prompting me to respond, "Refresh my memory."

Taking the seat next to mine, Andria started, *"Well...* we were waiting for Maverick to show up, drinking to pass the time. I told you to get his ETA, but you said you didn't wanna seem too pressed. So we drank some more, recorded one of those *Tik Tok* dance challenges, then I offered you pajamas to sleep here. But you insisted on keeping your dress on for whenever he showed up which clearly never happened since here you still are. Looking crusty as hell, might I add."

I honestly couldn't decide which part stressed me out more, the fact that I'd been filmed throwing aggressive elbows for *Tik Tok* or the part that equated to Maverick never showing up, a frown on my face when I asked, "Do you think he's okay? What if *something...*"

"He's fine, Camryn," Andria interjected, my eyebrow immediately piquing in response.

"How do you know?"

"I just do," she answered plainly, making me groan, "*Andria...*"

"Alright, alright," she conceded. "I know he's okay because he just posted on IG a little bit ago."

Since she'd intentionally left out what was actually posted, I decided to have a look for myself, clicking through the app until I landed on his profile and saw his most recent post that was one of those *iPhone* notes-style press releases that public figures seemed to love and I absolutely hated.

"She's just the homie. Relax. Damn."

From there, all it took was a quick trip to my gossip page of choice to see what that message was referencing, the picture of him looking super cozy with some girl at *Los Tacos* way earlier this morning making me roll my eyes as I muttered, "Exactly why I wasn't tryna be seen in public with his ass..."

The response he was getting was quite literally what I'd warned him about a few days ago to the point that I considered reaching out just to say "*I told you so*" until Andria asked, "That's all you're worried about? I mean, we're just gonna gloss over the fact that he went from *en route* to *in some other bitch's face?*"

Honestly, that part of it didn't really register in my head until she said it out loud. And while there was a split second of annoyance, *mainly with myself for ever entertaining his nonsense,* I quickly decided, "That was God's way of looking out."

If Maverick really had shown up, there was no doubt in my mind that we would've gone back to my place and spent the night racking up more regret for me to live with. But now, I didn't have to worry about any of that, ready to wipe my hands with the entire ordeal and glad to have Andria on my side once she agreed, "I guess it is Sunday."

MAVERICK

The internet was annoying as fuck.

Instead of nursing my hangover with Sunday brunch at my mother's house like I was supposed to be doing, I was stuck in bed dealing with the swarm of internet trolls coming at me crazy over one little picture. Hop, skip, and jumping to assumptions about shit when they knew absolutely nothing.

They never knew anything. Only the narrative created by gossip blogs which often sounded ridiculous in comparison to the actual truth that only the people involved would understand. But unfortunately, it didn't really matter since the lies always traveled a lot farther, a lot faster, leaving me to play defense; *again*.

The shit was honestly tiresome, tempting me to delete my account and never look back. But that idea only lasted a half a second since social media was where I made a good chunk of my money, and situations like this - *no matter how annoying* - were good for business.

Engagement was engagement.

Releasing a heavy sigh, I scrolled through the comments

of my latest post that were a mix of people attacking me for being out with Sophia and people attacking Sophia for being out with me. But the underlying theme was that we were both somehow wronging Lillian even though I was no longer with her and Sophia didn't even really know her like that.

The internet believed differently, though.

According to them, Sophia was a trash friend, *a back-stabber*, a ho who couldn't get her own man so she had to wait for Lilian's sloppy seconds which was wild to me since the truth was that Sophia had me first. Not officially, but we fucked with each other heavy. And that was the exact reason why Lillian had tried to paint the picture of them being friends on the internet, so no one would think anything of me being seen with Sophia one day and being seen with her the next.

She created this narrative that everyone was good with it, commenting "nice" things on every last one of Sophia's pictures that made it seem like they were tight. And because Sophia didn't care enough to make a point of correcting her, she went along with it; though I could only imagine how much she was regretting that shit now.

Tapping over to my texts, I was getting ready to send her an apology for my role in getting her wrapped up in all this mess until I saw my most recent text thread from last night.

"*Shit*," I hissed, sitting up a little too fast according to the way my head immediately started throbbing in response. But it was necessary since, *"How the fuck did I flake on round two with Camryn's fine ass?"*

She was really ready, too. I could assume she wouldn't have sent me an actual address if she wasn't. But not only had I stood her up, I'd also gotten caught out with another girl within that same timespan, surely making it look like I was just intentionally being an asshole.

Somehow, I already knew there was no coming back from that in Camryn's mind. But I had to at least try, typing and deleting a bunch of corny shit before settling on the truth.

"Sorry about last night. Got a little too faded and missed my ride." - Maverick

That was where it all started.

I was still inside the strip club when I requested the *Uber* I planned to pick her up in, the estimated time of arrival giving me a good ten more minutes of throwing ones before I was expected to be outside. But when that time came, I was already lost in conversation with Sophia who I'd bumped into on some random shit, happy to catch up with her since it had been a minute and we were both drunk as hell.

Running into old friends while drunk just hit different.

Unfortunately, all that drunk talk lasted long enough for my *Uber* to come and go. And by the time I grabbed my phone to request another, the battery was non-existent, leaving me stuck until Sophia suggested we go grab some tacos together.

Tacos while drunk?

Also hit different.

So my stomach and I instantly agreed to it, thinking nothing of it when she got us a ride to *Los Tacos* where we shared a few over more drunken conversation. But of course, now that some lame ass mothafucka had snapped a picture of us for the web and I'd fucked up any chance I might've had with Camryn, I wished I would've thought a little harder; even more so once I saw her reply.

"Who is this?" - Camryn

"Don't play with me, Cam. I fucked up. I'm sorry." - Maverick

Instead of responding with words, she only sent a thumbs-up emoji that somehow seemed worse than any lettered-response she could've given. And while I should've just left it at that knowing there was probably no coming back from the opportunity I'd tricked off, I couldn't help myself in trying now that I at least had her attention, once again typing and deleting a bunch of shit until I settled on a request.

"Can I make it up to you? Maybe over lunch?" - Maverick

Considering her reaction to my *Fatburger* suggestion the night before, I figured food was the best shot I had. But I quickly learned that a new day had sent Camryn right back to her old ways, a confused frown on my face once I read her response.

"There's nothing to make up to me, Mav.
Whatever happened was truly for the best." -
Camryn

"So you're not mad?" - Maverick

"Mad about what exactly?" - Camryn

Straight up outing myself felt like the wrong move. But
trying to play off what currently had the internet on fire was
virtually impossible, leaving me with no choice but to be as
direct as I could.

"Me not showing up. Being out with Sophia.
Hell, IDK." - Maverick

"Did your ego really come up with all that?
LOL." - Camryn

Her alleged laughs only made me more tense since I wasn't
messing around, a stance I defended in my next reply.

"Camryn, I'm being for real. I ain't no fuck
nigga." - Maverick

My mother hadn't raised me to ever be some intentionally malicious person. Even when I was wrong, I owned up. But none of that seemed to matter to Camryn according to her sarcastic response.

"Not a fuck nigga, and yet that's the descriptor YOU chose to umbrella how your actions could possibly be interpreted? Lol okay, Maverick. You got it." - Camryn

Going back and forth over text was starting to feel useless, especially since I knew it was a lot easier for Camryn to resist my charm when I wasn't in her face. So instead of continuing to defend myself, I suggested another in-person conversation that wouldn't require food even if I had plans to eat.

"Meet me at the office?" - Maverick

"Sure. On Monday morning. For work-related reasons only :)." - Camryn

"Not what you were saying the last time we were there..." - Maverick

She could act like it was a mistake all she wanted to, but I knew better than to believe that bullshit. Even with most of last night being a fog, I could still hear the enthusiasm of her moans, could still feel the intensity of her orgasms that lowkey made my dick hard just thinking about how fuckin' good it was to the both of us.

So good I didn't even bother pulling out.

Usually, that was the ultimate no-no. But Camryn struck me as the responsible type, meaning she wouldn't have let me go that far if she wasn't making sure we were good on the backend with some kind of contraceptive.

I wasn't worried about a baby. But I was worried about the possibility of never getting between her thighs again once I saw her definitive response.

"First and last time for everything, Mav. Now leave me alone so I can stop embarrassing you." - Camryn

"No shame in my game," I whispered to myself, getting ready to respond as such until another text came through.

"Your mama is looking for you, boy." - Mali

"Chill out with that boy shit. I'm headed that way now." - Maverick

A stretch of the truth, but the truth nonetheless as I powered my way into the bathroom for a quick shower so that I could wash off last night and get a fresh start with my two favorite girls. It was a tradition of ours to have brunch the last Sunday of every month, a check-in of sorts before heading into the next. And after a wild week between Lillian's rehab admittance, the gala, turning a corner with Camryn just to end up walking in a damn circle, and now this internet shit with Sophia, I needed it now more than ever, happy to be greeted by the sounds of old school R&B and the smell of biscuits fresh from the oven the second I stepped inside my mother's crib.

"Damn. I gotta get my ass back in the gym after all this eatin'," was my first thought as I curled into the kitchen to find my mother frying up some bacon and Malinda making herself a mimosa.

She offered me a premade one while teasing, "Social media, a thousand. Maverick, zero."

"Good to see you too, Mali," I groaned, holding my hand up to add, "And nah, I'm good. Had more than enough last night."

Honestly, just the sight of the champagne bottle made my stomach coil a little bit, giving me every reason to chill out on drinking for a minute. And Malinda only brought that point home even more when she asked, "Is that how you ended up at *Los Tacos* with ol' girl? Or was that just a publicity stunt?"

"If it was a stunt, I would've been prepared for the fall-out," I sighed, tossing an arm over my mother's shoulder for a hug before pressing a kiss to her temple. "How you doin', ma?"

"Would be better if I didn't have to wake up to my son getting dragged on the internet for the third time this week," she teased, clearly holding back a laugh as I groaned, "Shit, me and you both."

Finding a seat at the kitchen island, I continued, "It is

what it is, though. Just gotta let it blow over like everything before it."

That was the only good part about any of this.

Yeah, the shit was trash when it was happening. But the world moved so fast these days that I was sure the conversation wouldn't even last until the morning, *if* it even made it that long.

Of course, my mother saw it her own way, taking a swig of the mimosa that was originally for me before she replied, "That's all fine and dandy. But until you slow your ass down, none of it is gonna blow over fast enough for some nice young lady to take you seriously."

"Lillian took me seriously," I countered.

Though Malinda was just as quick to insist, "She said nice young lady."

The side-eye I threw her way in response didn't stop her from defending, "Come on, Mav. You know Lillian was "image" sweet. Not "real life" sweet."

My mother gave a look that suggested she agreed with Malinda. And while I couldn't exactly deny it since Lillian *was*… a complicated individual, to say the least, I still found myself defending her in her absence when I replied, "Damn. Kick a girl while she's down, huh?"

"I'm just sayin'," Malinda shrugged, completely amused until I flipped the topic back on the both of their single asses.

"Y'all all on my neck, but I don't see either of you tryna settle down with a nice man; young or old."

With a dismissive wave of her hand, Malinda groaned, "I'd rather mop the ocean."

"And I belong to the streets," my mother added, my eyes going wide while Malinda bust out laughing.

In fact, her laugh was so infectious that I couldn't help

laughing myself when I asked, "Mama, who taught you that?"

"The streets," she answered plainly, only making Malinda laugh harder as I shook my head while my mother managed to flip the topic back on us. "All I know is, I can't give myself grandkids. So one of y'all better get it together."

Malinda responded with a sip of her mimosa, proof that no babies were even on her radar. And while I didn't have the luxury of making a passive statement, I *did* have a valid excuse when I reminded her, "You don't like any of the girls I get with, but you still want them to have your grand-children?"

Wrinkling her nose, my mother responded, "Of course not. *Goodness.* The thought alone almost gave me a heart attack."

Chuckling at the way she clutched her hand to her chest, I insisted, "So then slow your roll, woman. We'll get there when we get there."

Her phone buzzing on the counter saved me from a tongue-lashing, the lift in her eyebrow giving me enough of a scolding on its own as she peeked at the screen before quickly excusing herself to take the call. And while I thought it was a little strange since she usually took calls in front of us, I tried not to make much of it until Malinda said, "Must be her new stray dog from last night."

My eyebrows furrowed. "*New stray dog from last night?* The hell did I miss?"

"Quite a bit since you were so busy making sure you stayed in Camryn's face," Malinda replied teasingly, giggling into her mimosa until I muttered, "*Camryn's face wasn't the only part of hers I got in last night...*"

That revelation made her choke on her sip. In fact, she was still coughing as she squealed, "WHAT?!" watching me for a reaction before she jabbed me in the arm. "Shut up! *Maverick...*"

"I know, I know," I replied with a big ass grin. "I almost couldn't believe it either."

Because Malinda was something like my best friend, I knew I could be real with her, the entire thing just as surprising to me as it was to her according to the way she was trying to make sense of it all.

"How the fuck...? *Why* the fuck...?"

Arrogantly, I explained, "*How?* On her damn desk. *Why?* Cause I'm a fine ass nigga with deep ass pockets."

That only made her roll her eyes. "So you paid for pussy? *Wow.* How original."

"No, I didn't pay for pussy, Mali," I answered with a laugh. "But my donations might've been the catalyst."

Wait.

Did I pay for pussy?

That question ran through my mind a second time after Malinda pressed, "Donations, plural?"

"Yeah, I threw her a little extra to make her day," I explained with a shrug, quickly concluding that that couldn't have possibly been the only reason Camryn threw me the box no matter what Malinda was insinuating.

I'd made her happy, and she wanted to show me how much.

It was a... culmination of sorts.

Not a moment, but *thee* moment where she finally let her guard down with me.

Finally let me have her.

"*Ugh,*" Malinda groaned, jabbing me in the arm again when she whined, "I really liked her, Mav! And she was doing so good avoiding your ass too. Now she's just... in the number."

"Don't say it like that," I insisted as I pulled out my phone to add, "And I'm sure you'll still like her after you see the cold ass shoulder she gave me this morning."

Scrolling to the beginning of the text thread between Camryn and I, I handed the phone over to Malinda to read, watching how every text that had me in my feelings earlier only made her giggle.

"Sis asked did your ego come up with that," she read out loud, the phrase smacking me just as hard as it had when Camryn first sent it. But it was also enough for Malinda to hand my phone back and conclude, "Okay, she's still good with me. But you better have used a condom, negro."

"*Mmhmm...*" I hummed, distracting myself with my phone to keep from having to say any more on the topic. But of course, it was my disinterest that only made Malinda more suspicious, leaning into my view to ask, "Maverick?"

"What?"

"Mmhmm? What does that even mean?"

"It means what it always means, Mali. Quit trippin'," I urged, keeping my eyes on my phone until Malinda snatched it from my hand and said, "Nah, this ain't sittin' right with the twinergy. So gon' ahead and tell me the truth."

Knowing she'd never let it go, I released a heavy sigh before I admitted, "I didn't use a condom. And I didn't pull out either. But Camryn seems like the type to be on birth control, right?"

"Probably should've asked her that question before you nutted in her, stupid," she scolded, using her free hand to gently smack me upside the head. "But to answer your question, I'm done making any assumptions about Camryn because I also assumed she'd never give you the time of day and here we are."

"You such a fuckin' hater, bruh," I groaned, giving real attention to my phone once it buzzed with a text while Malinda corrected, "Your favorite hater, *sis*."

Rolling my eyes, I glanced at the text, then at the number that wasn't saved in my phone, then back at the text as Malinda groaned, "I know that's not her texting you emoji eyes."

Shaking my head, I answered, "Nah, this gotta be Sophia."

Back when Lillian and I first got together, she'd made me delete Sophia's number. But the non-local area code told me everything I needed to know, a bit of a grin on my face as I matched her message with an extra set of eyes while Malinda asked, "She still wants a piece of your dumbass after dealing with that internet nonsense all morning?"

"I guess so," I told her with a shrug, watching the promising typing bubble pop up just as my mother returned to the kitchen. And while it should've been a priority for me to ask about the stray dog Malinda had mentioned earlier, I never got a chance to after my twin put me on blast once she announced, "Welp, mama. Looks like your grandchild wishes might be coming true sooner than we thought."

CAMRYN

F ood poisoning was kicking my ass.
     According to the internet, it was only supposed
     to last a few days at most. But here I was a solid two
weeks and change after an insomnia-induced *Los Tacos* run,
curled over the toilet at work trying not to throw my damn
esophagus up the same way everything else had been
expelled from my body.

Under any other circumstances, I would've just stayed
home. In fact, the first couple of days I was dealing with it, I
did stay home. But now, I was past the point of being able to
completely avoid work, trying my best to keep it together
even though, according to the concerned look on Meredith's
face, I wasn't doing a very good job.

Still, I tried to play it off, sipping from my glass of water
before getting back to the point I was making about our next
fundraising goal when I first excused myself. But I could
hardly make it through my entire presentation without
gagging, an act that embarrassed me even though, for whatever reason, it made Meredith giggle.

"Whew, I remember those days. Trying to make it

through a line on set while the twins were making their grand entrance into my body."

Regardless of how amused the memory had her, her comment still had me quick to explain, "Oh, no. I'm just dealing with a little case of food poisoning is all."

"*A little case?*" Janet asked. "Camryn, you've been sick for almost three weeks now."

"*Well aware,*" I thought, my stomach cramping as I defended, "It's a rare type."

It sounded reasonable to me, but Meredith didn't seem so convinced when she groaned, "*Mmhmm,*" before leaning in closer to advise, "I'd be getting in touch with that boyfriend of yours if I was you. What's his name? Nathaniel?"

"We're not together anymore," I stated firmly, annoyed that Nate had even been brought up. But I wished I would've just gone along with her suggestion once I saw the surprised look on her face after she put her version of two and two together a little faster than I could and whispered, "*Uh oh.*"

I knew I wasn't pregnant.

There was no way.

But Meredith's sureness was still enough to make me panic to the point of damn near hyperventilating, Janet putting a supportive hand to my shoulder in an attempt to calm me as she kindly asked, "Camryn, why don't you head on home? I'll get Meredith caught up on everything else."

"I'm fine," I defended, though a fresh cramp in my stomach told me to quit playing around.

A food poisoning cramp.

Not a baby cramp.

Either way - *or not, because there was only one way* - it was strong enough to change my mind as I told them, "On second thought, I think I'll take you up on that."

Janet still looked concerned as Meredith smiled on, catching me by the wrist on my way out to say, "Congratulations, sweetheart." And honestly, if she wasn't boss-equivalent around here, I might've punched her ass, the strained smile I gave in return saving the both of us as I dipped out of the conference room and speed-walked to my office to grab my things.

Because our receptionist didn't know what was going on, the way I was rushing back and forth around the office was enough to draw concern. But she waited until I was headed for the exit to actually stand up from her desk and ask, "Everything okay, Cam?"

"Everything's fine! I'll see you on Monday," I tossed over my shoulder, hoping to put her at ease that I was, in fact, not fired.

"But you might be after Meredith finds out who has you so sick," was the thought that flashed through my head as I strolled towards the parking lot; a thought I had to counter by defending out loud, "Yes, this is all Maverick's fault because his little incident at *Los Tacos* had me craving it for a week before I finally caved on the wrong damn night."

"Maverick did what now?"

The sound of his voice froze me in place, my eyes shutting tightly as I whispered, *"No fuckin' way..."*

Of course, once I turned around, there he was looking as good as he always did, a little smirk on his face as he bit into his lip before approaching me to ask, "You got my name in your mouth, but you can't respond to my texts? What's up with that?"

The smell of him was enough to make my stomach flutter, and not in the sick way that I'd been dealing with for over two weeks. More like, the pleasant kind of butterflies that made it feel like I was telling a story when I challenged, "Why would I respond to your texts if I have no interest in talking to you?"

Instead of being offended, he smirked to acknowledge, "You so mean," the little shrug I gave in return enough for him to continue, "You aight, though? You look a little sick."

"It's the food poisoning you overheard me blaming you for," I told him, not all that surprised when he frowned to ask, "Blaming *me* for?"

"Yeah, if you didn't have *Los Tacos* that night, it wouldn't have been on my mind," I explained, dead serious with my reasoning even though it only made him laugh.

"Cam, that was weeks ago," he reminded me like I wasn't well aware.

"Still your fault," I countered, getting ready to excuse myself until another wave of vomit made it to my mouth first.

Lucky for me, we were outside, so I didn't have to worry about making it into the toilet or trash can. But unlucky for Maverick, he didn't move out of the way fast enough, glancing down at the pile of throw-up near his feet where he realized, "On the Air Maxes, Cam?! Really?"

It wasn't *all* on his shoes. Just a few speckles from the splash of impact after it hit the ground. But it was still enough for me to feel bad, *emotionally and physically*, when I told him, "I am... *so* sorry. I gotta go."

My feet were already moving in the opposite direction by the time I heard him plead, "Camryn! Cam, wait up!" But I couldn't stop. Not until I was away from him and his mother's assumptions about my illness.

I was just sick.

Regular sick.

Getting sick was normal.

All of this was normal.

The only thing I needed to be concerned with was staying hydrated until it passed. But once I started feeling dizzy on my drive home, I realized that part couldn't wait, sending me on a detour to the nearest drug store so that I could grab a bottle of water.

Well... the water was what got me there. But once that was secured, I couldn't help taking a peek at the baby-making/baby-made aisle, trying to be lowkey as I scanned the assortment of products until I found what I was looking for.

"I don't even know which kind to get," I hissed, wondering if the generic, store-brand would give me the same accuracy as the popular kinds. But just as I went to pick one up so that I could read the back of the box, I heard a familiar voice call my name, my hand stopping in mid-air as I turned around and saw, "Nate. *Hey.*"

His approach made my heart race, quickly coming to the conclusion that it must've been fine nigga Friday since Nate *looked...* good enough to make me reconsider where we stood.

Bald head freshly shaved.

His facial hair cut low and neat.

A suit that I could guess was custom-made.

And those damn hazel-green eyes...

Nathaniel Bradford always looked good enough for a second chance.

And a third chance.

And a fourth...

"You got somethin' you need to tell me?" he joked, nodding at the shelf of pregnancy tests in a way that snapped my hand back down to my side.

"What? *No*. Of course not. I was just... picking up a test for a friend," I lied, giggling through my nervousness as Nate took a step closer. And now the intensity of my nerves was going off the scale as I tried to hide how sick I was feeling, my plastered smile somehow convincing enough for him to change the subject to the second bullet point on the list of things I didn't want to talk about.

Us.

Gently cupping my face, he stroked his thumb against my chin to say, "Can't believe you've been keeping this pretty ass face away from me, baby. I miss it. I miss you."

Typically, those words - *his words* - would melt me like butter. But today, I was practically freezer-burnt when I told him, "I'm more than just a pretty face, Nate."

"Oh, I know. I'm just sayin'. So damn *pretty...*" he trailed, bringing his lips closer to mine for a kiss that... a kiss I... a...

"Are you serious right now?" I snapped, snatching away to ask, "I haven't as much as spoken more than three words to you in months, and you think you can just pop up on me at the store and kiss me?"

Like it was nothing, he wiped his lips and shrugged. "I didn't exactly feel you resisting."

"That's not the point," I groaned, knowing my delayed reaction was simply out of shock. But now that I'd regained my bearings, I flat out told him, "We're done, Nate. You made that clear, and now I'm making it crystal."

For a second, he remained still, only pursing his lips together until they turned upward with amusement. Then he stepped forward to refill the space I'd created between us, pressing his body against mine so that he could look down at me to say, "Don't be like that, Camryn. You know you'll always be mine."

"Nate, I'm not about to do this with you right now," I sighed, pushing him away so that I could leave. And even when he reached for my arm, I yanked it out of his hold and growled, "Don't touch me," getting all the way to the end of the aisle when he reminded me, "You forgot your friend's test."

Stopping in my tracks, I released a heavy sigh before turning back around to grab one.

No, two.

"But three's probably the charm you need," I decided, tucking three different brands under my arm as I told him, "So she has options." Then I stormed off to the register to check out, pissed to find the line was long enough for me to have to stand there with three pregnancy tests and a bottle of water in my hand since it only added to the obvious of the tests being for me.

When I got to the register, the clerk took a glance at my purchases, then back up at me, then back down to the purchases before shaking her head, only making the entire thing even more uncomfortable as I stood there waiting for my transaction to be complete. But of course, she hadn't gone fast enough for Nate to not get another good look at me, the stress on my face surely giving him the truth about my situation even if I hadn't.

Oh well.

It was really none of his business either way. And it was really no big deal since I wasn't pregnant anyway, ready to get even the possibility out of my head so that I could focus on getting my health back to normal. But by the time I got home, I wasn't in the mood for anything other than a nap, opting to down the rest of my water and get some rest only to be awakened by the immediate need to pee a half-hour later.

"Should I take it now?" I wondered, the fact that I'd stored the pregnancy tests in the drug cabinet making it a little more convenient for me to grab one and stick it under my stream if need be. But when I finally got myself up to head to the bathroom, it was clear my bladder had other plans, its urgency forcing me to miss out on an opportunity that led to me avoiding the tests for the rest of the night and even into the weekend.

Monday ended up being the perfect time, though, since taking the test before work meant I could, *"I told you so,"* Janet who could then relay the message to her nosy sister. But the second I opened the cabinet door to grab one, all that confidence dwindled, only to be replaced with legit panic as I really considered the facts.

I mean, of course I didn't *think* I was pregnant. But there was also that one-tenth of one percent that made it a possibility; a number that grew exponentially when I thought about Maverick not using protection or pulling out. Then there was the whole thing of me being so busy with the gala - *and very inactive on the sex tip* - that my birth control hadn't seemed important. And because of my lack of birth control, my period hadn't been consistent, making it a little more difficult for me to figure out if I was even late or not.

Shit.

Releasing a heavy sigh, I knew there was only one way for me to put all this to rest. So I grabbed the test, removed the cap, pulled my panties down, and got the answers I needed in three minutes flat.

Not, not pregnant.

"What kinda ghetto shit…" I asked out loud, picking up the box to see it was the generic brand.

"*That's what my ass gets for trying to save a little money,*" I thought as I stood up from the toilet to grab another test. But when I sat back down, I realized I'd used all my good pee on the first test, forcing me to wait a few minutes so that I could get another stream going.

Thankfully, the fact that I'd been intentional about keeping myself hydrated over the weekend meant I wasn't waiting all day. But when the second test was complete, I realized I was going to need more pee cause… "*Pregnant?* Ain't no way in hell.*"

Tossing that test and its shady ass results to the side, I went for the third box that was going to set me free, this one requiring me to pee in a cup and set the stick inside for some seconds which I did while washing my hands. Then I pulled the test out and sat it flat on the counter like the instructions told me to do, waiting impatiently for the results to show I was, "Pregnant?!"

Anxiety settled in immediately, followed by the tears because… *what the fuck?*

How had I gone *years* of being careful only to get pregnant on the one and only time I'd slipped up?

That's all it takes, Camryn.

I knew that, which was why I'd always, *always* played it safe. But now, here I was, pregnant with Maverick's baby.

God, that made it so much worse.

If I would've slipped up with Nate, it would've at least made a little more sense, been rooted in some semblance of a relationship, *something*. But with Maverick, it was just a mistake that had turned into so much more.

Way more than I was sure I could handle.

The first person I got in touch with was Janet, shooting

her a quick text to let her know I'd be working from home today. The second was to Andria, breaking the news that I'd have to skip out on our plans to meet up for Margarita Monday without giving her all the details. And the third, most important text was sent to Maverick, still in disbelief that I was reaching out to him at all when I told him we needed to talk ASAP.

MAVERICK

F*ive new texts.*
Three missed calls.
One voicemail.

In comparison to the amount of notifications I usually woke up to, I considered this a pretty light load. But the fact that they were all from Camryn made it a little more interesting, though I could pretty much assume she wouldn't be trying to get in touch with me first thing on a Monday morning if it didn't have something to do with the foundation.

Or something to do with something I'd fucked up regarding the foundation.

Honestly, that wasn't how I was trying to start my day *or* my week. So I blew it off, instead choosing to focus on Sophia as she strolled into my bedroom wearing just my t-shirt, carrying a tray of breakfast tacos.

The girl was about to turn me into a damn taco since that seemed to be the only thing she ever wanted to eat. But considering the way she was throwing neck last night, I'd learn to love them if I had to, a grin on my face when I asked, "You really think you somebody's abuelita, huh?"

"Shut up," she giggled, setting the tray on the bed and following in behind it as she insisted, "I just like what I like."

Nodding, I smirked to agree, "And I like what I like too," pressing a little kiss to her cheek that made her blush until my phone started vibrating between us with another call from Camryn.

Peeking down at it, Sophia commented, "Your phone has been going off all morning. Is there somewhere you need to be?"

Knowing Camryn, it was more than likely less about where I needed to be and more about what I needed to do to be a better human since she loved to act like I was awful. And while I was sure my decision to ignore her in the moment would only give her the fuel she needed to really believe that shit, the way she'd blown me off for weeks before I finally gave up meant I didn't really care what she thought right now, giving a little shrug as I took a bite of my taco then answered, "Probably. It can wait, though."

Sophia was ready to agree with me until another text came through. "Are you sure, Maverick?"

Releasing a heavy sigh, I decided to take a quick peek just to see what had her blowing up my phone. And I was glad Sophia was too occupied with her taco to catch the immediate look of shock on my face once I read Camryn's most recent text.

"Since you've been ignoring me all morning, I have no choice but to tell you VIA TEXT that I'm pregnant." - Camryn

My heart dropped to my damn taco-filled stomach as I read the message again. Then I scrolled up the screen to see what her other texts had been about, only to discover a variety of pleas for us to meet up in person and talk ASAP.

"*Shit*," I hissed just loud enough to draw Sophia's eyes, trying my best to cover it up when I coolly suggested, "I uh... you should probably go. Cause I gotta go."

I was already out of the bed trying to find some clothes to put on when Sophia concernedly asked, "Is everything okay?"

"No," was the honest answer that blurted from my mouth before I could contain it, once again forcing me to attempt another cover-up. "I mean, yeah. Everything is fine. Just a... family emergency."

That wasn't exactly a lie since, if Camryn was deadass, I had a new family member on the way. But the broadness of my answer only made Sophia more concerned as she finally climbed out of bed and whined, "Oh no. I'll come with you."

She was already pulling her jeans from the night before back on when I held up my hand to stop her. "Actually, this is a family-*only* kinda thing. But I'll keep you posted, aight?"

Sophia wasn't usually one for confrontation, so I expected her to just nod and move on. But she didn't, instead standing firmly in place and crossing her arms to ask, "Is it her?"

"Huh?"

"*Lillian*," she clarified. "Is it her? Is that why you don't want me to come with you?"

If the situation playing out in my damn texts wasn't as serious as it was, I might've laughed in her face. But I couldn't even pull a giggle out of my ass, more annoyed than anything when I responded, "What? No, it's not her. I told you it's a family thing."

That wasn't good enough, Sophia getting right in my face to press, "Your mother? Your sister? Your aunt? Who is it, Maverick?!"

I couldn't even process her question, too focused on the fact that she really called herself raising her damn voice at me. But instead of letting that carry us into an argument I didn't really have the capacity to engage in right now, I stayed calm, gently grabbing her by the elbows to emphasize, "Now ain't the time, Soph. I really need to go. But we can talk about this later, okay?"

I was trying to be chill with her, but she didn't have any of that same energy for me, snatching away to shout, "I'm tired of playing these games with you, Maverick! Tell me who it is, or you'll never see me again."

Her demand made me chuckle, and not for good reason, my eyes tight when I asked, "I got a family emergency going on, and you choosing *right now* to be dramatic as hell? Never seeing you again honestly sounds like a bet."

It was crazy to say since I legitimately liked Sophia. We wouldn't have started kicking it again and she wouldn't have been in my crib if I didn't. But with the news that had just been dropped on me and the way she was acting, it seemed like a good time to cut my losses while I could, even if it meant Sophia spitting a strong, "Fuck you," in my direction on her way out.

I was sure I'd get a paragraph text from her about all this later tonight. But right now, my only priority was getting in touch with Camryn who, *of course*, flat out declined my first call.

The second one she answered, but not without making it clear how irritated she was when she asked, "Oh, so now that I told you what this was all about, you wanna call me back?"

"I'm sorry. I was busy," I told her, an explanation that wasn't exactly a lie even if she didn't care for it. Either way, it wasn't more important than figuring out, "Now what's going on?"

"I told you what was going on, Maverick," she replied annoyedly, forcing me to go down a line of questioning when she didn't immediately offer any additional information.

"And you're serious?"

The smacking sound she made with the back of her teeth told me everything I needed to know, even with her answering my question with a question. "You really think I would play about something like this?"

"*I just...* how did this happen? I thought you were on birth control?" I asked, realizing how wrong I was for assuming anything even though I was half-right according to her somber response.

"I was... until I wasn't. There was no need for it since I wasn't actively fuckin' anybody."

"So that means it's for sure mine?"

The question might've seemed insensitive, but I still had to ask knowing Camryn had been in an on-again, off-again relationship for as long as I'd known her. She could've easily gotten caught up in a double-back situation, an idea I found a little bit of comfort in until she replied, "Maverick, are you serious right now? You really think I'd want this, *with you*, if there was even a possibility that it wasn't yours?"

How she'd managed to give me an answer and fry my ass all at once left me a little stunned, though I still found room to defend, "I'm just asking, Camryn. I mean, *damn.* This shit is crazy."

Really, it was a step above crazy.

Something beyond my wildest imagination.

Camryn Cox, pregnant, with my *baby?*

It was clear the shock of it all was weighing on her even more than it was hitting me the way she exhaustedly sighed, "Tell me about it."

"And you're sure you wanna keep it? Cause I gotta be real with you, Cam. I don't know if I'm ready to be a father."

When she only responded with silence, I assumed she was taking some time to consider her options. But when that silence lingered a little too long, I asked, "Camryn? Camryn?" glancing at the screen only to discover she had hung up in my face.

"*What the hell?*" I asked, tapping to call her again only for it to go straight to voicemail. And when that happened a second time, I realized she was intentionally ignoring me; though that didn't keep me from trying to get in touch as I called, left multiple voicemails, and even sent a few texts that all went unanswered.

Fuck.

For a second, I thought about letting it go until whenever she was ready to talk. But after considering who I was dealing with, I quickly came to the conclusion that she could've easily held off on talking to me until the baby's first birthday - *or beyond* - forcing me to use the foundation's directory to find her address so that I could pull up on her.

Her car being parked outside of the complex was a good sign. But I still had to figure out a way to actually get into her secured building; particularly at off-hours when most people were already at work meaning there wasn't a lot of foot traffic going in and out of the main door. And just when I started to think it was a lost cause, God sent me an old lady who looked like she might need help with her groceries.

I couldn't get out of my car fast enough, trying my best not to alarm her when I asked, "Ma'am, can I give you a hand with those?"

The immediate look of shock in her eyes when she turned around told me I'd managed to scare her anyway. But with another blink, her eyes settled into more of an ogle, her lips matching the energy as she gladly handed me the reusable bag she was already holding and said, "The only thing your fine ass can help me with is the cobwebs covering my punani."

Her response was so unexpected that I choked on a laugh, accepting another bag of what must've been straight canned goods considering how heavy that shit was. In fact, I was starting to wonder how she'd planned to get it inside otherwise until I remembered I was supposed to be focusing on getting myself inside, maintaining my act when I told her, "I don't think my... *girlfriend* would appreciate that very much."

Referring to Camryn as my girlfriend was the kind of stretch she probably would've smacked me in the face - *or thrown scissors at me* - over. But I knew it would make this whole thing seem less suspicious for the sweet old lady who closed her trunk and asked, "Oh, your girlfriend lives here? What's her name?"

"Camryn."

"*Camryn... Camryn...*" she muttered before concluding, "Oh! You must be Nate then. It's a pleasure to finally meet you, handsome."

My immediate reaction was to frown since, *"Hell nah, I wasn't that nigga, and that nigga could never be me."* But again, in an effort to make things seem as normal as possible, I went along with it, giving a little nod as I answered, "Uh, yeah. Same."

Once we crossed the threshold of the secured area, I started looking around to see which way Camryn's unit was so that I could head in that direction the second I dropped the groceries off, grateful when the lady unknowingly gave me a hint after she commented, "I haven't heard y'all making all the noise you used to lately. Everything okay?"

With us being on the first floor, that meant Camryn's apartment had to either be on the left, on the right, or maybe even right above us if the lady had been able to hear her and Nate going at it. And while the thought honestly annoyed me a little bit, I did my best to play it off as I carried the groceries inside of her apartment while explaining, "That's actually why I was coming by. There's some things we need to talk about."

"Talk. *Right*," she playfully groaned, clearly hinting at the other kind of noise she must've overheard. But considering it was that that got us in this predicament in the first place, I knew that wouldn't be the case at all, mentally trying to prepare myself for what was sure to be a rough conversation as the lady moved closer to me to say, "Well, thank you for the help. I really, *really* appreciate it."

Her heavy hands were already planted on my chest by the time I realized what she was up to. And she was getting ready to slide them down my body until I stepped away with a weak, "You're welcome, ma'am."

From there, I couldn't get out of her unit fast enough, the fact that she was right on my heels forcing me to make a guess of going to the apartment on the left only to be met with a teasing, "Wrong way, Nate."

"Oh, damn. You're right," I laughed awkwardly,

heading back in the other direction as I joked, "See what happens when you distract me."

That made her smirk as she continued watching me while I knocked on the correct door, her attention remaining as I impatiently waited for Camryn to answer. And when I had to knock again under her watchful eye, I realized the only way I wouldn't completely blow my cover was by vocalizing, "Camryn. It's me. *Nate*."

Thankfully, that was enough to get Camryn to answer the door. Or... not Camryn, but somebody to answer the door, already in the process of telling me off when she started, "Nate, you got a lot of fuckin'... *oh*. Mav..."

"*Shhh*. Just let me in," I begged, giving a little nod to say, "The neighbor is watching."

Thankfully, the girl stepped aside to let me past. But once the door was shut behind us, she snatched me down by the front of my hoodie and whispered, "If Camryn finds out you're here, she's gonna lose her shit."

While I could assume her words to be true, it was the gesture that had me shook, frowning as I peeked down at her and asked, "Where is she? I need to talk to her. And who are you anyway?"

Loosening her grip just slightly, she growled, "Andria, her best friend, and the one who will gladly bust you in your shit if you came over here to start any more trouble than you've already caused."

Her solid, muscular build - *even on what couldn't have been more than sixty inches in height* - told me it was best that I take her words seriously. And I was just getting ready to hold my hands up and surrender when Camryn came from the back saying, "I know good and well I didn't just hear Nate at my... Maverick?"

Yanking myself out of Andria's hold, I firmly stated, "Camryn, we need to talk."

"About what?" she asked, crossing her arms over her chest to remind me, "You made your position very clear over the phone."

A lot of things had been said during that brief conversation. But I still didn't see the problem with the part that had actually made her hang up on me, using my own words to defend, "All I said was, I don't know if I'm ready to be a father."

"Should've thought about that before you shot the club up, nigga," Andria chimed in, catching a side-eye from me and heavy sigh from her friend who kindly suggested, "Andi, can you *just*... give us a second? Please?"

From the stern look on her face, I could tell she didn't want to. But out of respect for Camryn's wishes, she headed towards where Camryn was already standing, pressing a supportive hand to her friend's shoulder before shooting me a death stare on her way to disappearance.

Now it was just us. But with the way Camryn was looking at me in disgust, that didn't exactly make me feel any better as I approached her to explain, "Camryn, look. I was just being honest with you, letting you know how I felt in that exact moment. But that has nothing to do with me taking care of my responsibilities if you do decide to keep it."

No matter what, that part of things wasn't even a question. But according to Camryn, it wasn't really about that, a frown on her face when she countered, "Yes, letting me know how *you* felt without even waiting to learn how *I* felt about any of it. Questioning *me* without taking any responsibility for the role *you* played in all of this."

"You're right. You didn't do this alone," I quietly agreed

with a nod, grabbing her hands to add, "And I didn't mean to make you feel as such."

When she peeked up at me, I could see the distress written all over her face, her puffy eyes only making me feel worse for unintentionally giving her the impression that I was leaving her to deal with this by herself. But I suppose now that she knew I was right here with her, she felt more comfortable sharing, "I haven't decided yet. If I'm gonna keep it."

Thinking it might help take some of the pressure off, I suggested, "I know a doctor we can go to. If you're ready to discuss options."

"I already have an appointment scheduled with my regular doctor later this week, but thanks anyway," she replied, giving a shadow of a smile for the first time since I'd shown up until I asked, "Well can I at least come with you?"

Just like that, the shadow went away, a frown on her face as she sighed, "Maverick, I don't think that'd be a good idea. I mean, I'm not exactly ready for anyone else to find out about this, and you know the kinda attention you draw makes that virtually impossible."

"Which is why we should use my doctor," I insisted. "She's super private. And she even makes house calls if you need her to."

My impromptu commercial made her eyebrow pique with interest. "And you know all of this because?"

Shit.

By no means was this public information. But under these particular circumstances, it only felt right for me to be completely honest when I shared, "Lillian and I might've had a little situation we had to take care of a few months back."

The memory of that time was still fresh enough to give

me anxiety, remembering how sick I was when Lillian first hit me up to let me know she'd missed her period. But with her, the decision was easy and instant. She had no desire to be a mom, and I wasn't ready to be a dad.

She had her career that relied heavily on a picture-perfect image, and I didn't want to be the cause of her missing out on a bag.

So we made the calls, did what we had to do, and moved on like nothing had ever happened. At least, that's how we acted about it in the moment. But looking back on that time now, I realized things were never quite the same.

She was never quite the same.

Our normal partying and bullshit quickly began to turn problematic. Her drinking and drug use went from recreational to a full-blown addiction. And now, she was left to deal with all of that on top of what she'd gone through with the abortion.

Not that she regretted her decision.

I really think it was the process that left her scarred, steady trying to wash away the memories of that moment and the guilt that followed even though she'd done the right thing. And while I knew that wasn't the sole reason for how she'd ended up where she was, I still found myself mulling over the different ways I'd contributed to the problem until Camryn brought me back to the conversation with a simple, "*Oh.*"

Pushing me towards the door, she suggested, "On that note, you should probably go. But I'll um… be in touch?"

Nodding, I accepted her words because I had to, heading towards the door before turning around to assure her, "I know it's a lot, but we'll get through this, aight?" cupping her face to emphasize, "Together."

I held her gaze for a moment, hoping that would help to cue her in on just how serious I was. And while she seemed to receive the message, that didn't keep her from pulling away to rush me out of the door with a rattled, "Yeah, sure. Bye."

Somehow, her slamming the door in my face didn't feel nearly as bad as her hanging up the phone and then ignoring me, giving me hope that we really would get through this. But I could hardly process it all before the damn neighbor lady scared the hell out of me when she popped out of nowhere and said, "Well, that was quick. And no noise. Not a good sign, Nate."

Shaking my head with a chuckle, I continued towards the exit while telling her, "Find yourself some business, Miss. Lady."

"I'm tryna make you my business, suga!" she yelled after me, the fact that she was deadass only making me laugh again. But the second I got to my car and finally had a moment alone, *a moment of still*, all that amusement was lost as the reality of the situation really took over.

CAMRYN

"**W**ait. So you and Lillian Banks almost had project twins?"

Of everything Andria had overheard from the conversation between Maverick and I, somehow that was the first thing she wanted to talk about, the fact that Maverick was apparently so anti-safe sex that within a year's span, he'd accidentally gotten *two* people pregnant.

One of them was his actual girlfriend, who he loved and cared about.

And the other was me, who he just... wanted to have sex with.

Ugh.

"No, we didn't almost have project twins because if he would've had a child with her, there's no way in hell we would've ended up in this situation," I reasoned, tempted to blame their failed relationship for all of this no matter how ridiculous it sounded.

It was a fact, though.

I would've never, *ever* messed around with Maverick if Lillian had still been in the picture, Andria nodding to agree, "That's true. But I mean, she could be pregnant right now and because y'all didn't waste *any* time…"

Before she could finish her thought, I interjected, "Don't even put that in the universe, Andi! This is already stressful enough. And besides, I'm sure Maverick would've said something if that was the case."

He'd been completely open about their first secret pregnancy, so I couldn't imagine him keeping a current one under wraps until Andria challenged, "What if he doesn't know it's the case yet?"

Just the thought made my stomach hurt as I croaked, "Please stop."

"Okay, okay, my bad," she giggled like anything was funny. "But seriously, though. What's your move, Triple C? No judgment, just asking."

"Hell if I know," I sighed. "I mean, if you would've asked me two months ago if I wanted a child, I would've laughed in your face and called you a fool for even fixing your lips to pose that question. But now that it's drugstore pregnancy test real, I *just…* I don't know."

With the news being so fresh on my being, that was the most I could say about it without curling back into a ball and crying the way I'd been doing when Andria first showed up to my place. But just like in that moment, I was glad to have her here now to give me reassurance when she responded, "And you don't have to know. Let's just focus on getting you to that appointment in a couple days, and we can take it from there, okay?"

I nodded, we ordered in some lunch, and then I sent her home to finish the novel she was working on while I passed the time with a bunch of ridiculous documentaries on *Netflix*, grateful for the distraction until my stomach started hurting again.

Is it the food, or is it the baby?

The fact that I now had options only made me feel even sicker. But knowing there was nothing I could really do about it until I met with my doctor, I tried my best to ignore it - *to ignore the pregnancy, period* - acting like everything was all good when I finally showed up to work the following day.

And the next day.

But the third day, I found myself overacting, a ball of nerves as I spent less time doing actual work and more time thinking about the appointment I'd cleared my afternoon for.

Of course, because it was none of their business, I didn't have to disclose to my boss what said appointment was for. But that still didn't stop me from stressing myself sick about it, literally sweating under my pits when I realized it was only an hour before I was expected to be in the waiting room.

I thought I could do this alone.

That was the only reason I'd turned down Andria volunteering to come with me, insisting that I'd be fine when I sent her off to the writer's staycation she desperately needed to meet her deadline. But now that my appointment time was ticking closer and closer, I wished I wouldn't have been so convincing; especially when I realized there was only one other person it made sense to have accompany me.

Before I could talk myself out of it, I shot him a text.

"Hey. You busy?" - Camryn

"Nah, what's up? Everything okay?" - Maverick

His reply was almost instant, letting me know he really wasn't up to shit when I asked him for the same exact thing I'd turned down in person just a few days ago.

"Can you meet me at the doctor's office? For today's appointment?" - Camryn

"Of course. Send me the info." - Maverick

The first text I responded with gave him all the information he needed, and the second was more of a personal request.

"Also, can you be a little less... you?" - Camryn

It was honestly sad that I even had to ask for such a thing. But in this day and age where blogs paid good money for pictures of "celebrities" engaging in very personal shit, I knew it was the only way we'd maintain any privacy; though Maverick didn't exactly seem thrilled about it according to his response.

"Whatever that means…" - Maverick

Asking him to come fully disguised seemed a little ridiculous. But I knew giving him some sort of guidelines was the only way to prevent our business from getting out there, forcing me to come up with a list of things I thought might help our cause.

"Just be lowkey. Maybe wear a hat. No jewelry. Lay off the excessive designer print you seem to love so much." - Camryn

"So now you're telling me how to dress?" - Maverick

I was already typing out an explanation of how I didn't want either of us getting pictured when another text came through.

"I'm just messin' with you. I got you, mamas. See you soon." - Maverick

Why I found that so comforting, I wasn't sure. But it was just enough to get me to the doctor's office without passing out from stress, coincidentally pulling into the parking spot next to Maverick's G-Wagon that wasn't exactly lowkey amongst the cars of commoners.

I suppose it was better than his *Lamborghini* with the custom plates that would've easily outed him, the fact that he'd also taken my advice in dressing down making me feel a little better about inviting him until I got out of the car and heard him whistle in my direction.

His interest shouldn't have come as a surprise since I'd been intentional in my attempt at subscribing to the idea that when you look good, you feel good; giving my natural curls the attention they needed to really flourish, adding a little more color to my typically neutral makeup look, and taking advantage of all of my cute work outfits while they still fit.

The little things.

Showing his appreciation for my efforts, Maverick groaned, "*Gotdamn*. My baby mama fine as hell."

Stupidly, I blushed even as I cringed and scolded, "Don't you start."

"Just tryna help you relax," he insisted with a smirk, casually tossing an arm around my shoulder to guide me towards the entrance as he acknowledged, "You seem stressed."

The way he said it, you would've thought the circumstances didn't call for me to be completely freaked the fuck out, a frown on my face when I rhetorically asked, "Uh... can you blame me?"

Knowing better than to give an actual answer, he instead moved to stand in front of me, forcing me to stop and look up at him as he urged, "Chill, Camryn. I'm here."

His sentiment meant a lot, his presence too. But it also wasn't enough to keep me from holding a hand to my stomach so that I could counter, "You're also here. Chill deactivated."

I expected those words to be the reminder he needed to put everything back into perspective. But when he only responded with more ogling like he actually enjoyed that fact - *or just enjoyed looking at me, period* - it was me who got the reminder of who I was dealing with, giving him a little push to the chest as I blew past him with a groaned, "Will you stop?"

"Ain't my fault you lookin' all extra good today," he defended as we continued inside. "Reminding me how we ended up here in the first place."

The thought alone made me roll my eyes, mad at myself for such a huge lapse in judgment as I told him, "You're disgusting."

"You didn't seem to mind it," he fired back arrogantly, knowing I couldn't deny his claims if I wanted to since... *well,* that *was* how we got here. But instead of giving him the satisfaction with my agreement, I focused on getting checked in for my appointment.

At least, that was my plan until the medical receptionist didn't even glance my way when I approached the desk, so focused on Maverick that I had to clear my throat before announcing, "I'm here for an appointment with Dr. Strong. Camryn Cox."

Like I'd snapped her out of her lust-filled daze, she shook her head a little bit before sliding a clipboard my way to instruct, "If you two will just have a seat and fill these out for me. One of the nurses will be out to take you back shortly."

She finished her spiel with a slick smile in Maverick's direction like his ass wasn't clearly here with a pregnant woman, the whole thing annoying the hell out of me as I snatched the clipboard and rushed to find a seat as far away from the desk as possible. But even as I penned my answers on the medical history form she'd provided, I couldn't shake how bothered that interaction had me.

I mean, it wasn't like Maverick had entertained it, or that he couldn't entertain it since it wasn't like we were together. But the fact that she'd been so bold with her attraction made it hard for me not to ask, "Do women always look at you like that?"

"Yup," he answered plainly. "All of them except for you. *Well*... outside of that fateful night."

Again, I rolled my eyes. "Are you trying to annoy the shit out of me? Or is this really just your natural state?"

For whatever reason, my obvious diss only made him chuckle. "Come on, Camryn. You know me."

"*Unfortunately,*" I muttered, handing the clipboard his way so that he could fill out the information regarding his own medical history. But as I peeked over his shoulder with plans to only preview what boxes he was checking, I realized just how much I *didn't* know about him.

His birthday.

His address.

That he was apparently allergic to peanuts.

In fact, I was getting ready to ask him about that one until he blurted, "It's a coping mechanism. Joking around to manage the stress of all this. I mean, I would've never thought *that* would turn into *this*."

If it hadn't happened with me, I would've thought he was an idiot for not considering the possibility; especially after his situation with Lillian not all that long ago. But in reality, I felt the same way. I mean, of course I knew how sex worked and that it was possible even with proper precautions. But I also knew the very particular timing and circumstances it took to conceive a child, two things that were far in the back of my mind when Maverick was sexing me senseless on top of my desk.

Shit.

Flashback.

Swallowing hard, I finally replied, "Yeah. Me neither."

"I'm glad you hit me up to join you, though," he mentioned with a smile, grabbing my hand to add, "It would've killed me to let you go through all this by yourself."

Maverick was a touchy-feely person by nature, so I shouldn't have thought anything of the gesture. But in the moment, I couldn't help myself, absorbing the brief sense of peace that came with his support when I agreed, "I'm glad you could come."

"Even when I'm annoying the shit outta you?" he challenged, his acknowledgment making me smirk as I sighed, "*I mean*, that part could obviously be taken down a notch or twelve, *but…*"

Before I could finish, a nurse called my name, Maverick guiding me towards the secured doors with a gentle hand against the small of my back that I was sure had homegirl at the front desk tight. But really, it wasn't about her at all, just having Maverick here to back me period making everything seem a little less intimidating.

He was patient as I got examined and went through all the different testing, happy to answer the questions Dr. Strong had for him and even supplied a few of his own. And when he could tell I was becoming overwhelmed, he did everything he could to help keep me calm.

Imagine… Maverick Woods… keeping me *calm.*

It was like I was experiencing an entirely different side of him; a side that I was quickly growing fond of as Dr. Strong concluded we were five weeks along. And while I could pretty much assume that from the timeline of events and the last period I could remember, putting an actual number to it brought a sheen to Maverick's eyeballs that caught me completely off-guard.

"You okay, Mav?"

Swiping a hand down his face, he gave his beard a tug

while answering, "Yeah, I'm just… *wow*. Five whole weeks. That's crazy."

Crazy was honestly the understatement of the year, seeing Maverick get all emotional about it making me emotional as I did my best to hold in the tears that came with hearing Dr. Strong very thoroughly explain the different options we had in terms of how we wanted to proceed.

Parenting, abortion, or adoption.

Only one felt right to me, but I didn't want to let the emotions of the moment override every other thought I'd had over the last few days. And I was glad Maverick agreed, being the one to tell Dr. Strong we'd get back to her as soon as we'd made a decision before we were sent on our way.

Again, I didn't want to get caught up in the emotions of it all, didn't want to impulsively do anything I'd live to regret for the rest of my life. But with everything still so fresh, now felt like the best time to discuss it, the fact that we were still in public leading me to suggest, "I haven't eaten lunch yet. Should we grab some food and head back to my place? Talk through this together?"

Running a hand against the back of his neck, Maverick avoided my eyes while answering, "*Umm…* I actually have somewhere I need to be. But we'll talk soon, aight? I'll hit you up."

The change in his energy had me confused, my eyebrows furrowed as I slowly nodded and agreed, "Okay." And in no time at all, he was back in his truck while I remained standing outside of my car, trying to make sense of where sweet, supportive Maverick from the doctor's office had gone.

Maybe he really did have somewhere to be, or maybe he just needed some time to process it all alone. But there was also this nagging third idea that had me feeling silly for getting caught up in his act so easily, quickly coming to the conclusion that while it was nice to experience another side of him, to temporarily feel his comfort and support, Maverick only being worried about Maverick was his default setting.

MAVERICK

Five weeks.

So much had happened in that time that you could've told me it had been double the amount and I would've believed you. But nah, in the span of five weeks, I'd broken up with my girlfriend, had sex with the girl I'd lowkey dreamed about, dated and undated a chick from my past, and now had a baby on the way.

A real ass, Dr. Strong-confirmed ass baby.

If I wasn't me, I would've thought the nigga involved was trash. But being that nigga, I knew it was a little more complicated than that simple classification since my situation was Lillian was literally a matter of life and death long before I pulled the plug on our relationship, messing around with Camryn wasn't something I could just pass on, and hooking back up with Sophia had been a direct result of Camryn playing me off.

Okay, so maybe I was a bit trash for that part. But with Sophia being so open and available, I couldn't help myself, preferring to keep some company around instead of ever being completely alone.

Growing up with a twin, I never really had to be. But once Malinda started doing her own thing, I had to find my way, only to get caught up in the fake sense of companionship that came with being in the spotlight.

There were always people around, but I still felt lonely more often than not. I was popular as hell, had all the followers, but I had very few ride-or-die friends that I could count on for whatever. And even when people did come into my life that I thought had my best interest at heart, it didn't take long for me to realize that most of them just wanted to come up off being associated with me, making it even harder to decipher who was real and who was not.

With women, it was a bit different, though. Even if they were trying to come up, they still played the role of really being there for you, giving the kind of companionship I was after that made me care a little less about their original intentions. And eventually, it would all start to blur together anyway, feeling real enough for me to find comfort in even when it wasn't exactly rooted in the truth.

That's how it was with Sophia and I, an exact replica of that fake shit turning real dynamic until I fucked it off for Lillian's aggressive ass who wouldn't take no for an answer. And while that should've been the first clue that we wouldn't make it in the long run, we'd still managed to fall in the kinda toxic ass love that ended up in biopics decades later.

Man, I was glad she was getting some help; even more so now that I had my own situation I was dealing with. And with that on my mind, I couldn't even participate in my usual Thirsty Thursday shenanigans, knowing there was too much potential trouble involved with being out in public right now.

Home was the only place my ass needed to be.

Of course, just because I wanted to stay home, that didn't mean there weren't a bunch of people hitting me up to come out, tagging me in different events that were happening around the city and literally begging me to pull up. Even my boy Whoa hit me up about an event he was DJ'ing at locally, the most tempting offer of all but still one I had to pass on since there was way too much on my mind.

At the doctor's office, I'd done my best to be strong for Camryn, being there for her such a huge priority that I'd put my own feelings about it all on the backburner until Dr. Strong dropped that number.

Five weeks.

Somehow, even after all of the examinations, and the questions, and the testing, it was that moment that made it all real for me, bringing literal tears to my eyes as I thought about how those five weeks could really be the beginning of a whole new world for me if Camryn chose to keep the baby.

But did I want her to keep it?

With Lillian, I hadn't really been involved in those moments, staying as disconnected as possible from it all since I already knew what the outcome would be. But with Camryn, things were just different, making it even more confusing for me to know where I really stood.

I was going back and forth about it in my head as my phone continued to buzz with a variety of notifications, every glance at the screen making me more annoyed until I picked it up to find an incoming *Facetime* call from my sister.

Tapping the screen to answer it, I waited for the video to connect before I asked, "What you want, Mali?"

"Is that really how you greet your sister?" she asked with a frown. "What's the matter with you?"

Releasing a heavy sigh, I scrubbed a hand down my face and lied, "Nothin'. My bad. What's up?"

"Your little friends blowing up my phone is what's up. They sayin' they can't get ahold of you. Why is that?"

"Cause I'm not really in the mood to talk to anybody right now," I answered with a shrug, hoping Malinda caught the hint that that included her too.

She didn't, nodding to agree, "That's fine," before probing, "But also... what's going on? Seriously?"

Even with her concern being legit, I still sighed. "Just a lot on my mind, Mali."

"Which puts a lot on mine thanks to our twinergy. So spill it."

Of course she could feel something was bothering me. And now that she could see me, I knew she wasn't going to let it go, making it harder for me to come up with some story regarding my mood as she waited for me to explain.

So instead of even trying, I got the truth off my chest, putting a neat little bow on it when I finally shared, "There's a strong possibility that I'm gonna be a father come Christmas."

There was no immediate reaction from her side, making me wonder if the call had frozen until she leaned in closer to the screen and quietly asked, "I'm sorry, what?"

"You heard me, Mali."

"But you didn't say nearly enough, Maverick," she insisted, her eyes tightening as she questioned, "A father? To whose baby?!"

Now that part I really couldn't speak on, completely respecting Camryn's wishes of keeping everything under wraps when I answered, "I can't tell you all that right now."

"Maverick Carter Woods don't make me pull up on

you," she threatened like that was somehow going to change my mind.

In fact, I had to chuckle a little bit as I replied, "You can pull up all you want to, but I still ain't sayin' shit."

My response was enough for her to fall back from that plan, taking a different route to the answers she was after when she sighed, "Goodness, Mav. All that hoe shit you've been on, I can't even imagine what kinda girl is on the other end of that positive pregnancy test."

While me being on "hoe shit" was debatable since it wasn't like I was out here just fucking any and everybody, it did feel good to be able to defend, "Trust me. I could've done a lot worse."

Sure, Camryn wasn't my girlfriend or anything like that, but she had her shit together. She was independent and ambitious. Feisty when necessary, but also extremely caring when it came to the causes she spent her life's work on. And my mama already adored her, a badge most of the girls I dated never even came close to claiming.

Just from that sentiment, Malinda deduced, "Well that knocks Lillian off the list of possibilities. And I know it's not the taco girl cause y'all haven't even been kicking it long enough for her to be... oh shit!"

"What?" I asked, her exclamation making me sit up in my seat as I watched her lips turn upward into a knowing grin.

"It's Camryn, isn't it? You got Camryn Cox pregnant?!"

For a second, I thought she was using the twinergy to read my mind for real until I remembered discussing it with her a few weeks back at brunch.

She would've never been able to draw that conclusion if I would've just kept my mouth shut. But now that she'd yelled it loud enough for the gotdamn world to hear, I could only groan, "*Ahh, fuck.*"

"Maverick, oh my goodness!" she squealed, clearly amused when she continued, "That's... *wow*. I'm truly speechless."

"Good. Stay that way. Cause you're not even supposed to know any of this shit," I warned, glad that she was calling me from her apartment since that bettered our chances of this conversation actually staying between us and us only.

For how long, I wasn't sure. But for now, Malinda was at least able to give me her word when she assured, "Out of respect for her, I'll stay quiet. But wow, bro. *Wow.*"

"I know," I agreed with a nod. "Shit is crazy."

That was the word I kept coming back to; *crazy*. Though Malinda's mind was still stuck on the words I'd used to make my initial announcement, one eyebrow raised as she asked, "Why do you say a strong possibility, though? I mean, if she's pregnant, she's pregnant."

"We haven't had the talk yet," I explained. "Made a decision of what we wanted to do."

"Is she really considering all options? Or is this just Lillian part two?" Malinda questioned, the mention making her realize, "Damn, Mav. That wasn't even half a year ago!"

"Trust me, I'm well aware," I sighed. "But as far as I know, she's considering everything. Like I said, we still need to talk."

With how heavily everything was weighing on me now, I should've been making that a priority, Malinda once again reading my mind twin-style when she asked, "Well what are you waiting on?"

"I *just*... needed some time to think on my own. The doctor's appointment had me feeling shit I ain't never felt before, and I didn't wanna let that one emotional moment charge me up for some shit I don't know if I'm ready for."

That was the honest truth of why I'd gotten out of there the way I did, knowing a discussion with Camryn in that moment would've had me hopping online to order a *Burberry* shirt for the baby shower. But now that a little time had passed, I felt better equipped to answer Malinda when she pressed, "So how are you feeling about it now? Do you want her to keep it?"

"*I mean...* I'm not as against it as I thought I was when she first told me she was pregnant."

Somehow, that was enough for Malinda to conclude, "Oh my God, I'm gonna be an auntie!"

"Can you be any louder, though? *Gotdamn*," I groaned, frowning at the screen as my sister issued an apology.

"I'm sorry, bro. I'm just so excited for y'all."

Maybe if it was a sure thing, I'd be hyped too. But considering who I was dealing with, I knew better than to even allow myself to feel that, giving Malinda the same advice when I told her, "Well don't get too excited. Cause knowing Camryn, the baby could already be an afterthought."

"Don't say that!" she exclaimed. "Sure, all of this probably has her terrified. But I still don't think she would do something like that without at least letting you know."

"Guess there's only one way to find out," I sighed, the grin on Malinda's face telling me everything I needed to know as she offered me her support.

"Good luck, twin. Let me know how it goes."

"Yeah, aight. I got you," I agreed before ending the call, mindlessly tapping into my *Instagram* app only to be smacked in the face with the last picture I needed to be seeing right now.

"God, you did that on purpose, huh?" I asked out loud, unable to hold back the smile that came naturally from just looking at the pretty ass selfie Camryn had recently posted. The curls from earlier were pulled up into a ponytail at the top of her head, her face was still mostly made-up, and the fire dress she had on at the doctor's office had been replaced with an oversized "Hillman College" sweatshirt, giving her this relaxed yet somehow still sexy vibe that had all her homegirls gassing her in the comments under the picture she'd captioned, **"Gilbert Hall Legend"**.

"Yessss, friend. You fine, fine!"

"Let me borrow that sweatshirt, though."

"You better give us a casual lewk, sis!"

"You tryna be the Whitley to my Dwayne or nah? Touch-down???" was the comment I typed and deleted knowing Camryn would've swiftly cussed my ass out about it. But I still continued to admire the picture, already imagining which features our son or daughter would inherit from her and which ones they'd get from me.

"Yeah, this shit was definitely a set-up," I decided as I clicked over to her profile, skimming the mix of selfies, softly-filtered shots with her friends and family, and then photography-style pictures of random items she found intriguing.

The shit was ordinary as fuck, but somehow still gave off

this warm vibe that had me grinning as I started thinking about her collection possibly including me.

Including our kid.

Including our family.

Did she want that?

I honestly wasn't sure.

But one thing was for certain; I was ready to make my case for why she should.

CAMRYN

Sunday brunch just wasn't the same without a mimosa.

I was trying not to let it get to me, trying to be happy that I was at least able to keep my food down. But with every sip that Andria took from her champagne glass in celebration of meeting her deadline, I felt myself growing more and more jealous, wondering how the hell I was going to survive thirty-five more weeks of this.

Thirty-five more weeks.

According to the estimated due date Dr. Strong had provided, keeping the baby meant I had thirty-five more sober weeks of pregnancy left. Thirty-five more weeks until I could meet my daughter or son, and thirty-five more weeks of navigating new waters with Maverick until both of our lives would be changed forever.

We still hadn't talked about it.

In fact, I hadn't even heard from him since we left the doctor's office a few days ago. But I could pretty much assume that, *like me*, he was still trying to process it all, trying to draw his own conclusion on how he wanted to proceed the same way I'd drawn mine.

I wanted to be a mother.

Of course, I didn't envision it happening as a result of these particular circumstances. In fact, the way I saw it happening was almost exactly opposite of the way it had all gone down.

I was supposed to meet someone, fall in love, get engaged, become a wife, then enjoy marriage for a few years before we decided it was time to bring a child into the world. But instead, I'd had a one-night stand with a man who'd charmed me straight out of my panties and now had me carrying his child.

No love.

No marriage.

Just baby.

Yeah, I really could've used a mimosa to swallow down that harsh reality.

Luckily, the end result of all of this would still make one of my ultimate dreams come true. And for that reason, I was trying to find the good in it, a genuine smile on my face when I asked Andria, "Give me your early prediction. Girl or boy?"

Sneaking a bite of her breakfast potatoes, she gave a few chews before concluding, "I gotta see how you're carrying first. Then I'll decide."

"Hopefully, you won't be seeing anything for at least a few months," I thought out loud, glancing down at my stomach that was still sitting like normal. Not quite flat, but not squeezing uncomfortably against my jeans either. The happy medium that would be completely demolished whenever Baby Cox-Woods decided it needed more room to grow.

Or maybe just Baby Cox depending on what Maverick had to say about all this.

Like she could read my mind, Andria asked, "So when are you and Maverick supposed to talk?"

"Whenever he hits me up," I answered with a shrug, stabbing at what was left of my waffle as I thought about the possibility of that happening a lot later than sooner.

What if he'd already decided he didn't want me to keep it and was just delaying correspondence so that he could find a nice way to put it?

What if he was waiting to hear back from the same doctor he and Lillian had used so that he could be prepared to suggest we take that same route?

What if he was working behind my back to get me fired so that he didn't ever have to face me and take responsibility at all?

Just the thought had me pulling my phone from my purse to shoot him a text, only to discover there was already a message waiting on me.

"Can you come over? So we can talk?" – Maverick

He'd sent that about twenty minutes ago, around the same time our food was delivered which meant I certainly wasn't paying my phone any mind. But now that I'd already left him waiting a little while, I was curious to see if his request remained the same.

"Come over when?" – Camryn

"Whenever you're free. I'll be here all day." - Maverick

Maverick, *at home*, on a Sunday Funday?
    No brunch?
    No day party?
    No post-church sinning?
    Truthfully, I was a little concerned, already bracing myself for the worst as I typed out a response.

"Send me your address. I'll swing by in a little while." - Camryn

Once I had the information I needed, I cut brunch short by a few minutes, ready to get this conversation out of the way so that I could start planning for whatever was next. But when I showed up to Maverick's place, it seemed like staying in the moment was just as important since... *why is he so fine, though?*

That had never been my first thought when it came to Maverick. At least, not in recent times since him being in my face was typically a result of some annoying shit. But the longer I stared at him, the more I was starting to think the baby was responsible for making me more attracted to him as he nodded towards my hand to ask, "What's in the bag?"

"Leftover chicken and waffles," I answered, slipping past him into his apartment as I explained, "I didn't wanna leave it in the car, but I'm probably not even gonna eat it. You want it?"

Like I'd asked an offensive question, Maverick frowned. "I can't be takin' food out of my child's mouth already. Not until we get to the fruit snacks stage."

"Your child doesn't even have a mouth yet," I giggled. "At least, I don't think it does."

Now I was the one frowning in thought, tempted to pull out my phone and do a quick *Google* search to see if the baby looked like anything more than a blob by this point until Maverick asked, "You feelin' okay?"

The fact that I was actually standing upright meant I was doing better than I thought I'd be. But I still wasn't sure if "okay" was the right classification for how I was feeling, releasing a sigh as I told him, "As well as I can be. You?"

"I'll be better once I know where your head is at with all this," he replied, giving a bit of a grin as he finally accepted the food I'd dropped on his countertop.

His nice, quartz countertop that only added to the surprise of his apartment being tastefully decorated.

I mean, of course there was the giant seedy sectional couch and the bigger than necessary television that was a staple in all bachelor pad living rooms. But he also had a nice rug, and dope art on the walls, and throw pillows that actually tied in with his aesthetic and weren't just the extras from his bed set.

Well... that I actually couldn't confirm. But it looked like they'd been purchased with intention which was enough for me to compliment, "I gotta say, this is not at all what I was expecting your place to look like."

Plating the food so that he could warm it up, Maverick explained, "I have two very important women in my life who refused to have me out here looking crazy."

Now that made more sense; though I could still give him credit for maintaining the look even when I teased, "Only two?"

I was confident Lillian had had her hand in something around here. Hell, probably Sophia too. But I wasn't pressed about it, glad that Maverick knew to take it as a joke when he simply responded, "You're funny" before turning around to put his food in the microwave.

Since there was nothing else for me to do, I watched intently as he set the timer with two pushes of the thirty-seconds button. Then he turned back around and gave me his signature look; the flirty, ogling one that he followed up by asking, "Why you lookin' all good today? Where you comin' from?"

As if the food I'd just given him didn't make it obvious, I answered, "I went out to brunch with a friend."

"*A friend?* So I'm about to eat the chicken and waffles that another nigga paid for? You cold-blooded, Cam."

Giggling at his assumption, I watched him pull the plate from the microwave before it could actually beep. Then, without waiting a second for it to cool - *or even adding some hot sauce* - he went straight for the wing, ripping it with his teeth in a way that allowed me to counter, "I see that's not stopping you, though."

"Shit, it's already warmed up now," he shrugged, holding his bone in the air to give a directionless, "Thanks, bruh."

Shaking my head, I explained, "For your information, I paid for both me *and* Andria to eat because she met her deadline."

"Well that's good for her mean ass," he groaned, the fact that he was clearly still scarred from their first interaction making me giggle as I defended, "She's not mean, she's protective. There's a difference."

"Sure, Camryn. If that's what you gotta tell people to keep your lil' strong-handed friend out of jail," he insisted, stuffing an oversized bite of waffle into his mouth and groaning in response to the warm maple syrup it was already coated with before poking at another bite.

It was honestly distracting to watch him greedily devour my leftovers, his enthusiasm reminding me of when we were back at the office and he was giving my pussy that same attention. But knowing that was exactly how I ended up in this situation, I shook my head so that I could appropriately respond, "Nah, she doesn't do the jail shit. She has boy cousins for that."

Nodding, Maverick continued to eat until his plate was clear a literal few seconds later, the fact that I could've easily made a meal of what he'd treated like a snack leaving my eyes wide when I asked, "Damn, Mav. Did you even chew?"

"Shit was good as fuck," he groaned, moving to rinse his plate and get rid of the trash while asking, "What I gotta do to have you treat me to brunch the way you treated your homegirl?"

"I don't know. Accomplish something," I answered with a shrug, confident that it would be a while before I'd even have to think about taking him anywhere until he shot a heated glance over towards my stomach. "That doesn't count."

"*With you?* It definitely counts for something," he insisted with a smirk, taking the counter opposite of mine to continue, "But um, speaking of that. How would you feel about…"

Before he could even finish, I interjected, "I'm keeping the baby, Maverick."

I didn't want him to think he could change my mind, didn't want him to think I'd come over here to be convinced of anything. I knew what I wanted, and I was firm in that decision regardless of how much he planned to be involved. Though I had to admit, I was surprised to hear his sighed, "*Thank God…*"

"What?"

Taking a step forward, he closed the space between us, grabbing my hands to explain, "If you would've just let me finish, I was going to ask how you felt about keeping the baby."

"Seriously? I mean, you want that?" I asked, legitimately shocked as he went on to say, "I gave it a lot of thought over these last couple days. And while I know the circumstances aren't ideal, I just… *yeah*. I want that, Camryn."

The little smile he finished with told me he was serious, and I should've been relieved to hear that he was in this with me; that I wouldn't be doing this alone. But before I could allow myself to really feel any of that, I had to ask, "Why, Maverick? Why do you want it? Why now?"

Considering how things had gone when he and Lillian were in the same predicament, I couldn't understand what had him so confident this go-round. But instead of giving me the answers I desperately needed to hear, he confusedly responded, "Why are you asking me that like you've suddenly changed your mind?"

"I haven't. *I just…* why are you so sure this time? Why with me?"

Asking that question caused a lump to grow in my throat; emotions that I wished I could blame on the extra hormones from the baby but knew better than to lie to myself about since the truth was, I really wanted to know.

What had him so certain that this was the right thing to do?

What was so different now in comparison to a few months ago?

Why was he so interested in taking this journey with me? So okay with the idea of being connected to me for the rest of his life when he could've easily been pleading his case for the exact opposite?

Lifting his hand to cup my face, he licked his lips before quietly answering, "Because I know you'll be the mother our baby deserves. And I'm ready to match the energy."

Maverick touching me so tenderly should've been my cue to move. But I didn't, instead meeting his stare until he brought his lips down to mine to seal his words with a literal syrupy-sweet kiss that had me floating onto my tippy toes.

The fact that I'd fully embraced the gesture only encouraged him to take it a step further, lifting me onto the countertop where he slid between my legs and let me know exactly where our kiss was starting to affect him. But before I could make good use of his erection, his phone started buzzing near my ass, snapping me back to reality when, instead of ignoring it, he immediately picked it up and hissed, "*Shit.* I need to get this."

Knowing it was probably for the best, I gave him a nod that told him it was alright to take the call, mainly so I could get my ass out of this compromising position. But once I heard him address who was on the phone, it felt like the sign I needed to remind me that this wasn't going to be any less complicated just because Maverick was onboard.

He still had a lot going on outside of our baby, mainly all the social media shit and the blogs who made a business out of being in his. And I could only imagine how much more complicated that was all getting ready to become once

I overheard him ask, "You want me to come visit you in a couple weeks? They're allowing that already?"

Of course, I couldn't hear what Lillian's response was. But from the look on Maverick's face, I could tell he was really considering it which was enough for me to leave before I started to insert my feelings into a place where they did not belong.

Did kissing him confuse things?

Obviously.

But the fact of the matter was that even though Maverick was the father of my unborn child, he was not my man.

It was time for me to start acting accordingly.

MAVERICK

Our second doctor's appointment was completely different than the first.

With Camryn inching up on the eight-week mark, we were now eligible for all the things that made the baby even more real.

The first ultrasound.

Testing for any potential birth defects.

Hearing the heartbeat.

For as stoic as Camryn had been towards me since our conversation back at my apartment when we'd decided we were keeping the baby, I was glad to see that part crack her facade, a single tear slipping out of her eye in reaction to the peanut on the screen and the unbelievably fast heart rate that was somehow music to my ears.

Baby Woods was doing great.

The parents, on the other hand…

Things between Camryn and I had strangely gone back to normal.

Like, before the sex and the baby normal.

Our communication was mostly about random shit with

the foundation. Our interactions were limited to the office. And even with this appointment, she'd only sent me a *Google* invite like it was a damn business meeting or something, keeping everything hella professional like we were co-workers instead of parents-to-be.

Maybe that was what she wanted; for us to approach this as co-parents with no actual emotional attachment to each other. But being real with myself, it was a little too late for that.

I mean, I couldn't look at Camryn carrying my child without imagining a world where we ended up together. I couldn't see myself being platonic friends with the woman who was now thirty-two weeks away from blessing me with the world's greatest gift. And I certainly couldn't get comfortable with the idea of being demoted to court-approved hours and a monthly check while another man got to be in my child's life full-time as a result of being in a relationship with Camryn.

That shit already had me hot just thinking about it, legit jealous of an imaginary nigga that I knew I could eliminate by giving Camryn every reason to see things my way. And while I was confident that she wouldn't make it easy for me, I was too motivated to let that deter me, making my first move when I wiped the tear from her cheek and shot her a grin to let her know I had her back.

The smile she gave me in return was a bit strained. But I could assume that had less to do with me and more to do with the heavy emotions of the moment, the entire thing hitting a bit different now that she could actually see what was growing inside of her.

A raspberry with a heartbeat.

Shit was crazy and fascinating all at once, knowing something so tiny would soon be changing my life forever.

And from the astonished look on Camryn's face as she stared at the monitor, I could tell she was thinking the same thing; a beautiful sight that warmed my chest as Dr. Strong wrapped up the appointment before sending us on our way with a prescription for prenatal vitamins that were covered by insurance and a keepsake sonogram.

Since she'd only given us one that was left in my possession, I asked Camryn, "You want me to make you a copy or somethin'?"

"Make *me* a copy?" she repeated with a frown like I'd asked a stupid question. "How about you give me mine back, and I'll make *you* a copy?"

"Who said this one was yours?" I challenged, the fact that it was still in my hand giving me a little leverage until Camryn responded, "You mean, besides it having my name on it, being paid for with my insurance, and being of my literal insides?"

With that, I knew I had no choice but to hand it over. Though I did feel a little better about it once she shared, "I'm gonna keep it in the baby book."

"That'll be dope. But before you do that, let me get a quick picture first."

She didn't seem thrilled about the idea, but she didn't fight me on it either, holding the sonogram against her folder of information for me to snap a picture of with my phone while warning, "If this ends up on your *Instagram*, I swear to God I'll get a restraining order."

"Now why would I do some silly shit like that?" I chuckled, looking through the photos I'd taken to make sure I had a good one as she continued to stare me down. "*Wait.* You really think I'd do that?"

She shrugged. "I wouldn't put it past you. And for good

reason, Mr. *'Post a selfie right after my girlfriend was admitted to rehab'.*"

"Ex-girlfriend," I corrected. "But it's funny that you mention that since I'm actually going to visit her in a couple days."

Even though I was pretty sure she'd overheard me talking to Lillian about it on the phone before she'd stormed out of my apartment a few weeks back, I wanted to be straight up with Camryn so she wouldn't think I was trying to sneak around on her. Though, judging by the way she immediately frowned in response, I was wondering if I should've just kept that shit to myself.

"And you're telling me this because...?"

"Because I want you to be able to trust me when I tell you I'm only visiting her as a friend," I explained, feeling confident in my ability to do so until Camryn stopped in her tracks to ask, "Does she know that?"

"*Honestly?* I'm not sure," I admitted. "But I plan to make it clear if she doesn't."

Of course, there were concerns about how well Lillian would take the news if she really was hoping for some type of reconciliation. And I could only hope that her program had something in place for her to deal with it healthily since it wasn't my intention to set her back, the whole thing lowkey starting to concern me until Camryn gave me something new to worry about when she started walking again and insisted, "I guess it doesn't really matter anyway. I mean, it's not like we're a couple. You can visit her on whatever terms you want to."

The nonchalance in her tone was so forced that I couldn't help but laugh. "See, that's the thing. You say that, but I don't think you really mean it."

That stopped her again, a frown on her face when she crossed her arms over her chest and asked, "Excuse me?"

"You'd really be okay with me getting back with Lillian? In the midst of all this?" I questioned, getting close enough to make her really take some time to consider her answer.

Avoiding my eyes, she pushed out, "I didn't say that. I just know you're a grown ass man who's going to do what he wants to regardless of how I feel about it."

"But how *do* you feel about it?" I pressed, gently resting my hands against her waist as I watched her struggle between what she wanted to say and the truth.

Biting into the corner of her lip, she started, "I feel like... you already know the answer to that question." Then she peeled herself out of my hold, tossing a casual, "I'll see you around, Mav," over her shoulder on her way to the car.

Somehow, that felt like progress.

No, she wasn't completely on board with the two of us pursuing an actual relationship. But to me, it didn't seem like she was totally against it either. And really, that was all I needed to feel like I had a shot; though I also knew none of this shit would be right if I left too many loose ends untied.

It was time to put a knot in the Lillian situation.

———

"Oh my God! You have no idea how happy I am to see you!"

As if Lillian's squeals weren't startling enough, watching her do a little jog in my direction so that she could jump into my arms for a hug made everything even more... *uncomfortable?*

Strange?

Inappropriate as fuck?

I honestly wasn't sure what the correct word was for it. I just knew it didn't feel quite right. But considering I wasn't about to embarrass her for no good reason, I let her have her moment, being serious when I responded, "It's good to see you lookin' healthy."

The weeks before Lillian was admitted were, by every account, rough as hell. So to see her all bright, and airy, and sober, and even a little thicker in some places brought a genuine smile to my face as we found a table to share, Lillian insisting that I hold her hand as she replied, "If nothing else, they've kept me well-fed in here. But how are you? How is everything out in the real world?"

"Honestly? Enjoy your time away from it all. Cause the real world is just as crazy as you remember it," I sighed. "I mean, it's been weeks since we broke up, and your fans are still coming at me on some wild shit online."

For whatever reason, that made her giggle. "Can you blame them? They loved us together. Hell, *I* loved us together," she emphasized before quietly adding, "Still do."

The way she said it had me quick to pull my hand away so that I could tell her, "Lillian, I don't want this visit to confuse you. I'm only here because I still care about your well-being, as a friend."

"Oh. *Right.* Of course," she sighed, playing it off with another laugh as she gave a little wave of her hand to change the subject. "*Anyway.* Tell me what's been going on with you? What's new?"

On one hand, I didn't want to make any of this about me; wanted to keep the conversation about her and her progress. But on the other hand, I knew now was as good of a time as ever to get the truth off of my chest even though I was sure Camryn would kill me if she knew I was sharing it.

There was only so much longer we'd be able to hide it,

though. And for that reason, I felt a little more confident telling Lillian, "*Well...* I recently got some life-changing news. Something you should probably hear directly from me instead of finding out from someone else."

"Uh oh. Who's pregnant?" she asked with a laugh, her energy and the question both catching me off-guard. And I suppose she could sense that from the surprised look on my face since she knew to continue, "Come on, Maverick. You and raw sex go together like peanut butter and jelly, so who is it? Sophia? You know, I read about you two in one of the gossip magazines a staff member slipped me."

"They shouldn't have done that," I scolded. "But actually, no. It's not her."

"Damn. These bitches work quick," she said amusedly before casually asking, "How much are you paying her to get rid of it?"

Shaking my head at her assumption, I frowned and answered, "Nah, it's not that kinda situation."

Now Lillian was the surprised one. "*Wait.* So she's keeping it?"

The slow nod I responded with was enough to turn her speechless, her eyes wide as she struggled to find the words. "Wow. That's... wow, Maverick."

Sitting back in my chair, I gave her a second to process, watching her expression go from shocked, to somber, and finally the anger that had her speaking through clenched teeth when she leaned into the table to say, "We were together for almost a year, and you campaigned for me to get rid of our baby. But you're keeping the baby you made with some random?"

Instinctively, I sat back up so that I could defend, "First of all, she's not a random. And second of all, campaigned? You didn't want to keep it either."

I honestly wasn't sure why she found it necessary to rewrite history, but I knew the truth. And she did too, which is why she switched up her approach by insisting, "If you would've asked me to, I would've, and you know that."

"I *didn't* know that," I corrected. "But you know we weren't in any position to raise a child anyway. You had your career, *and…*"

"And I would've given that up for our baby," she interjected, appearing to be on the verge of tears when she quietly added, "I would've done anything to make you happy."

The long, intense stare that followed was enough to break me out of character, my lips slowly turning upward into a grin as I complimented, "I see you still got it."

"And I see you still make the best improv partner," she replied with a smile of her own, wiping away the crocodile tears she'd worked up as she shared, "My manager already has a few sympathy roles lined up for me when I make it out of here."

"You don't need the sympathy. Your skills speak for themselves."

I mean, if I didn't know how she operated, I would've surely believed every bit of what she was just saying about the baby. But it was good to see that even with everything she had going on, she was still sharp in her craft, blushing to reply, "I appreciate that," before continuing, "Real talk, though. Please do right by that child, Maverick. I know what it's like to be raised in a broken, toxic home, and I wouldn't wish that on anyone. Especially not an innocent little baby."

"You have my word," I assured her, pulling my phone from my pocket so that I could show her the picture I'd taken back at the doctor's office. "Here's the first ultrasound from a few days ago."

Sliding the phone her way, I shouldn't have been surprised when the first thing she commented on was, "Camryn Cox, huh?"

"You're supposed to be looking at the baby, Lillian," I groaned, watching as she zoomed in on the fuzzy blob while also asking me, "Why does that name sound so familiar, though?"

"Probably cause she works for the foundation," I explained, that fact making Lillian's eyebrow pique with curiosity.

"Oh, so you were serious about it not being a random?"

"You thought I'd lied about that?" I asked, a little offended as she slid the phone back my way with a shrug.

"I mean, considering how quickly everything happened, I just couldn't imagine any other scenario."

It was a fair explanation since the timing of it all was definitely suspect as hell. But I was glad to see her taking the news in her own special version of "well"; grateful to see the genuine smile on her face when she grabbed my hand to say, "I really appreciate you coming today. And I know you're going to be the best dad and an even greater husband."

"*Husband?*" I asked, not sure what that had to do with anything until Lillian explained, "I tried to throw you a bone a few times and you didn't even take a nibble, which means Camryn must be something special."

That I couldn't deny, even if I still wasn't sure how I was going to get Camryn to believe me. But I was willing to put in the work, for now focusing on the conversation at hand that ended with me telling Lillian how proud I was of her and her advising me to stay persistent with Camryn.

"*What an interesting turn of events,*" I thought as I hopped into my whip to head back to the city, the drive giving me some time to think about what being persistent with Camryn even looked like.

I didn't want to come on so strong that it turned her off, but I also didn't want to leave any room for confusion - *or another nigga* - meaning I couldn't exactly pace myself.

Nah, it was a full steam ahead kind of scenario. And that's why I called myself rushing home to take a shower so that I could go pay her a visit, getting all the way dressed only to discover some trouble once I picked up my phone.

"#YOULOVETOSEEIT An anonymous source sent us this picture of Maverick Woods reuniting with Lillian Banks at her treatment facility earlier today. Not only is our girl looking good and healthy, but it appears that getting clean has also helped her get her man back!"

I hated this shit.

Like, literally despised that not only had someone completely invaded our privacy by taking a picture of us in a damn rehab center of all places, but they'd also decided it was a good idea to run to the internet with it, surely coming up on a few bucks just for sharing it with the gossip blog who knew they'd get a lot of attention for having an exclusive.

Except... it wasn't really an exclusive since it wasn't the truth. But of course, nobody cared about that part, the comments already filled with people trying to dissect every piece of what they were seeing.

"OMG! Look at how they're looking at each other. They're definitely still in love <3"

"Awww, they're even holding hands! Love them!"

"Is it just me, or does it kinda look like Lillian was crying?"

See what I mean.

If this was really any of their business, they would know the slight puffiness in her eyes was all an act. But instead, it was turned into us having some deeply emotional conversation that ended in happy tears because we were officially reconciling.

All of that... from one picture.

As always, I was tempted to clear the air before people started planning our post-rehab wedding. But for some reason, it felt more important for me to reach out to Camryn first; to let her know that I'd kept my word in making sure my visit stayed platonic even though the internet was saying otherwise.

Assuming she'd already seen it for herself, I got straight to the point with my text.

`"Camryn, I promise you that picture is not what it looks like." - Maverick`

It took a minute for a response to come through, long enough to have me expecting some paragraph of a text. But to my surprise, Camryn only responded with the single letter that somehow said just as much without saying anything at all.

"K." - Camryn

"K? That's it?" - Maverick

"Yes. Okay, Maverick. Whatever you say." - Camryn

Reading between the lines, I could tell it wasn't as simple as she was trying to make it out to be. And even more obviously, she wasn't taking me for my word, something that frustrated me since I knew I was telling the truth.

"You really don't think I'm being honest with you, do you?" - Maverick

"Truly don't care either way." - Camryn

Using my knowledge from a couple days ago when she'd said something similar, I felt confident calling her out.

"That's a lie and you know it." - Maverick

"The same kinda lie as that picture not being what it looks like, right?" - Camryn

While it was slick of her to try and throw it back on me, I was still annoyed that she was getting caught up in the hype instead of really hearing me out, something I couldn't help questioning her about in my response since I could almost guarantee this wouldn't be the last time some shit like this popped off online.

"So you really gonna believe the internet's narrative over mine? The actual person in the picture?" - Maverick

"You really gonna act like you wouldn't believe your own two eyes if you saw a recent picture of me holding hands with my ex?" - Camryn

Just the thought had me feeling a way, a scowl on my face as I typed out the only response that mattered.

"Fuck that nigga." - Maverick

"Finally. Something we can agree on." -
Camryn

Releasing a heavy sigh, I decided it was time to take a fresh approach in getting her to believe me, tapping out of our text thread so that I could call her on *Facetime.*
Was it risky?
Hell yeah.
But I knew her being able to see my face and hear the sincerity in my tone might be the thing to help me turn the corner. *Well,* at least in the event that she actually chose to answer the phone.
Once I saw the call connecting, I assumed it must've been my lucky day; especially after catching the easy smile on Camryn's lips when she asked, "Can I help you with something, Mr. Woods?"
Damn, she looks good.
Her curls were in this half-bunned, half-down situation that gave off this innocent vibe like she wasn't just frying my ass over text. And with that in mind, I tried to stay focused instead of letting her cute ass distract me, licking my lips before I answered, "Yeah, you can by telling me what I gotta do to make you believe Lillian and I weren't on some romantic shit. I know the picture looked extra friendly, but she was really just showing her appreciation for me being there as her friend."
Her smile remained, but I could still tell from her tone that she was being sarcastic when she replied, "I'm sure that meant a lot to her since it's clear *you* still mean a lot to her."
"She knows I've moved on," I clarified. "She knows everything."
It took her a second to catch what I really meant by that.

But once she did, all that sarcastic shit flew out of the window, a scowl on her face as she asked, "Mav, I haven't even told my damn parents about the baby yet, and you thought it was a good idea to tell your ex?"

"She's not gonna say anything," I assured her. "I just felt like I had to say something so the news wouldn't catch her off-guard and set her back in her program."

To me, it was a noble thing to do. But to Camryn, it was just another bullet point on the list of things that annoyed her, her eyes rolling as she groaned, "How thoughtful of you to consider how *she* might feel about *our* personal business."

"I feel like you're being sarcastic again."

"You should," she responded plainly, letting me know the conversation wasn't at all going as I'd intended it to.

Still, the fact that she hadn't hung up in my face meant there was a small chance for me to recover. So instead of wasting any more time and letting things get even further off track, I came as correct as possible when I told her, "Look, Camryn. I'm really not tryna upset you. I just thought reaching out to you directly would mean a lot more than some general write-up for the folks on the internet. Us being good in real life is way more important to me than whatever a bunch of strangers wanna believe."

Regardless of how she chose to receive my truth, I was happy to be able to get it off my chest. Though I can't lie, it felt good to see the tiny smirk on her face when she replied, "I appreciate you calling, Mav. Now if you don't mind, I'd like to get back to the movie you've been interrupting for the last twenty minutes."

"Movie night without me? That's fucked up."

Of course, I was only playing with her, trying to take advantage of her better mood by keeping things light. But to my surprise, she was the one to take it a step further than that, biting at the corner of her lip before suggesting, "Maybe we can... set something up, for another time."

"Yo, you for real?" I asked, watching her give a bashful nod that had me way too hyped when I told her, "Shit, I can pull up right now if you want me to."

"I said another time, Maverick," she repeated with a giggle, forcing me to find some chill as I nodded and agreed, "Aight, aight. I'll let you get back to your little movie then."

Giving a friendly wave towards the screen, she ended the call shortly after, leaving things between us on a good note until I realized...

Wait.

Did she really mean that, or was she just trying to get me off the phone?

Knowing Camryn, it was easy for me to believe the latter. But knowing myself, I wasn't about to let her get away with vocalizing plans she didn't intend on keeping.

That movie date was happening whether she was serious or not.

CAMRYN

I 'd officially run out of excuses.

Maverick had been pestering me for weeks now about the movie night idea I'd thrown out on a whim just to get him off the phone. And while I'd always had a "valid" reason to postpone things to a later date - *sick, work, exhaustion, random other plans* - tonight, I had nothing.

My pregnancy sickness had mostly tapered off.

The project I'd been giving most of my attention to at work was now complete.

I was tired, but that wasn't going away any time soon.

And now that my stomach was beginning to harden and the only other person I'd told about the baby was busy with her own shit, making Friday night plans with people meant possibly sharing the news that I still wasn't quite ready to make public.

Not that I was regretting my decision or anything like that. But I knew telling my girls I was pregnant meant them asking for more details, mainly who the father was. And that shit was *just...* too messy right now; especially with most of the world believing Maverick had reconciled things with Lillian even though she was still in treatment.

For him, it was much easier to just let the next trending topic steer the public's attention elsewhere than to try to change people's minds. But that still didn't mean people suddenly forgot about them as a couple, which would only make me something like another Sophia in the scenario.

Sophia, but with child.

Thinking of it like that almost made me sick all over again. But because I knew the truth - *that this baby wasn't conceived while he was in a relationship with anyone else, Maverick and Lillian were just friends, and I was no Sophia* - I was able to swallow it down and focus on responding to Maverick's text asking me what food I wanted him to bring over for our date.

Or is it a date?

Maverick hadn't made it sound overly romantic whenever he brought it up. More like the two of us just getting a chance to hang out and get to know each other a little better now that we'd decided to bring a child into the world. And considering I would've definitely shaded any man trying to make our first date a basic ass movie night at my apartment, I could only hope that wasn't his intention. Though I suppose under these particular circumstances, it was actually kind of perfect.

Since we wouldn't be out in public, I didn't have to worry about us being seen, wouldn't have to worry about popping up on someone's gossip blog or being attacked by Lillian's fan club. And because he was just coming over to eat and watch a movie, I didn't have to spend a bunch of time getting cute; the ultimate plus, especially after putting in a request for a medium pineapple and pepperoni pizza that I didn't plan on sharing.

"Is that a typo or you really like that nasty shit?" - Maverick

"Nasty?! Have you ever even tried it, Mav?" - Camryn

Of course, I was used to the non-believers who were more grossed out by the idea of fruit on pizza than the actual pizza itself. And according to Maverick's response, he fell into that same group.

"Hell nah. Cause the shit's gross." - Maverick

"But how do you know it's gross if you've never had it?" - Camryn

"Cause I have eyes. Anything else you want me to pick up?" - Maverick

While there was nothing physical I needed him to grab, I still had a request to put in, already giggling to myself as I typed out a reply.

"Yes. Better taste." - Camryn

"Have you seen the woman carrying my child? My taste is just fine :)" - Maverick

"*Cute,*" I said out loud, blushing a little bit as I brushed off the compliment he always seemed to have for me as of late.

"Annnnyway. I'll see you in a few." - Camryn

After seeing Maverick's response of the "okay" hand emoji, I left my phone alone so that I could take a quick shower. Not because I had to be fresh for Maverick's arrival. But because my boobs were sore as shit and in desperate need of some extra relief after being in a bra for the entire workday.

The hot water helped a lot.

A little massaging did too.

And by the time I found some shorts, panties, and a sweatshirt to put on, it was already decided that the bra was getting left out of the mix and Maverick would just have to deal.

Honestly, I couldn't imagine a scenario where he didn't appreciate my boobs being free. But after catching the faint sounds of his voice as he talked to someone in the hall, I realized I'd be finding out the truth soon enough, a smirk on my face as I put my ear to the door before opening it just in time to hear my neighbor say, "Good to see you again, Nate. And don't forget what I told you."

Frowning, I watched Maverick use his free hand to give a

little wave as he responded, "Alright now, Miss. Lady," before slipping into my apartment with a casual, "What's good wit' you, mamas?"

Instead of answering his question, I posed an important one of my own. "Why the hell does my neighbor insist on calling you Nate?"

"She thinks I'm him," he replied like that was at all normal, setting two pizzas and a grocery bag down on my counter as he shared, "It's actually how I got into the building the last time I was here before you gave me the door code; by playing your ex."

While I could appreciate him being resourceful, I still groaned, "That's disgusting."

"More disgusting than Miss. Lady telling me she better hear some noise comin' from your apartment before the night is over?" Maverick challenged with a smirk as I squealed, "Oh my God! She said that to you?!"

Shrugging, he only made matters more embarrassing when he added, "Said I ain't been hittin' it right lately. That I need to step my game up."

"How would she even know that?" I questioned, really curious about just how much she'd heard back when Nate and I were together as I continued, "And besides, according to this stomach of mine, you knocked it out of the park on your very first time up to bat."

For whatever reason, that brought a huge smile to Maverick's face as he repeated, "Stomach? You felt the baby kick or somethin'?"

Shaking my head, I answered, "No, it's still a bit too early for that. It's just… getting really tight."

"Lemme see," he insisted, slipping both of his hands under the front of my sweatshirt to touch my almost baby bump.

"According to the app I use, eleven weeks means the baby should be about the size of a lime," I explained, trying to ignore the flutters that came with having Maverick's hands resting so intimately against my bare skin. But the longer they remained, the harder that became; especially when combined with the look of admiration in his eyes that was enough for me to quietly ask, "What is it, Mav?"

"Thank you," he sighed affectionately, finding my eyes to repeat, "Just thank you."

"And thank *you*... for bringing this food," I told him, pulling away to emphasize, "Specifically, my delicious pizza."

Now he was the one shaking his head, unpacking the grocery bag that I now knew was filled with movie candy as he groaned, "Can't believe you really about to feed that to my baby. *The disrespect.*"

"Just try a little bit, Mav," I insisted, offering up a bite of the slice I'd already grabbed that he dodged with an enthusiastic, "Hell nah."

"Come on. Just a bite," I pressed, practically shoving it into his mouth before I asked, "Good, right?"

Begrudgingly, he chewed it, giving an exaggerated swallow that already had me giggling by the time he replied, "Just be happy I didn't spit that shit out."

"Oh, whatever!" I squealed, making a plate of three slices while Maverick did the same. Then we headed to my living room, Maverick doubling back to the kitchen to grab us something to drink as he asked, "Aight, so what we watchin'? Somethin' old? Somethin' new? Somethin' blue?"

"Somethin' blue?" I repeated, giving it some thought before offering up the only one I could think of. "Like *Avatar*?"

"Nah, that movie is way too long," he answered,

handing me a glass of water and setting his own onto the coffee table while suggesting, "What about that one on *Netflix*? About the nigga and the wine?"

"That's what I was watching when this whole movie night thing first came about," I told him, picking up the remote so that I could scroll through our available options. "What about *Bad Boys For Life*? I never did make it to the theater to see it, but I think it's available to rent now on *Amazon Prime*."

"Saw that already," Maverick answered through his mouth full of pizza. "What else they got on there, though?"

Continuing to scroll, I stopped when I saw, "Ooh, how about *Queen & Slim*? That's another one that left theaters before I could go see it."

For whatever reason, that made him chuckle. "Camryn, what *is* the last movie you went to see in theaters?"

"The last one I saw? Or the last one I can remember seeing?" I questioned, only making Maverick chuckle harder as I defended, "It's not my fault everything goes digital so fast these days."

"That's true," he agreed. "But there's nothing like being at the theater with the comfy, reclining seats, some fresh popcorn, and a cherry Icee."

While I could only imagine how much time Maverick had spent in that exact predicament between his mother and his ex, it still wasn't enough to change my mind when I replied, "I'm just fine with my couch, my pineapple pizza, and the adult beverage I would be drinking if it wasn't for your determined sperm."

"You're welcome," he teased, earning himself a mean side-eye before I pressed play on the movie that had my full attention while I was eating. But once I had nothing to keep myself occupied, it became a struggle to stay awake.

Not because the movie was boring. In fact, that was far from the case. But the fatigue that came with growing a baby was a different kind of beast that had me waking up mid-sex scene to ask, "*Wait*. How did we get here? What did I miss?"

"Almost the whole damn movie with your sleepy ass," Maverick joked as I sat up from my slouched position under his arm to remind him, "Again, if it wasn't for your... *goodness*, they are really gettin' it in."

"Looks familiar, huh?"

"Shut up!" I squealed, unable to take my eyes away from the screen as the scene flashed to something totally different. "Okay, now who is this little boy? And why is he at this protest?"

"You slept through his introduction," Maverick answered, giving me no additional information that might've helped me understand what I was seeing as it flashed back to the sex.

"But why are these two scenes happening at the same time? What is going on?" I asked, legitimately confused as Maverick groaned, "Camryn, will you just watch the movie?"

Since it was obvious he was fed up with my questioning, I'd missed too much to know the answers myself, and the sex *was*... honestly starting to make me feel some things, I figured now was a good time for a bathroom break, hopping up from the couch to tell Maverick, "I need to pee."

"Want me to pause it?"

Giving a little toss of my hand that he couldn't really see since I'd already passed him, I replied, "No, you can keep watching. I'll be right back."

"You sure?" he yelled over his shoulder, loud enough for me to hear from the bathroom doorway. And while I could appreciate how courteous he was trying to be, I still told him, "Yeah, it's fine. I'll have to rewatch the whole thing later on anyway."

"Later on" really meant within the forty-eight-hour rental period since I was definitely going to get my money's worth. But considering that was more information than Maverick needed right now, I finally peeled into the bathroom, taking a long pee and reflecting on everything tonight had already been.

Sure, I'd slept through a bit of it. But in the time I'd spent awake, things between Maverick and I had been incredibly... *comfortable*. Almost as if it wasn't our first time kickin' it like this. And when I came back from the bathroom to find Maverick's arms stretched across the back of my couch, that point about comfortability was only reiterated since it was clear he'd made himself right at home.

Strangely enough, I didn't mind it. In fact, I kinda liked it; was admittedly enjoying having him around. But considering this was supposed to be us just casually hanging out, I knew I had to pump the brakes, taking the first step in doing so when I returned to the living room and took the opposite end of the couch.

Instead of keeping his eyes on the movie, Maverick glanced my way to ask, "Why you sittin' all far away now? Come back over here."

"I only cuddled you in my sleep by accident," I told him, assuming that had to be how I'd ended up under his arm since I couldn't remember exactly how it happened.

Either way, Maverick didn't care, quick to insist, "Well now I want you to cuddle me on purpose."

When I didn't rush to move, recognizing it as the thing I'd intentionally been trying to avoid, Maverick grabbed my hand and urged, "Come on, Cam. You know you were comfortable as hell all tucked up under me. And I was comfortable having you there."

There goes that word again...

Truthfully, I *was* comfortable there.

Too comfortable there.

But now that he'd admitted how he felt about it too...

Before I could overthink things any more than I already had, I blurted, "Maverick, is this a date?"

Even though I was being serious, he responded with a laugh. "Is that a real question, Cam?"

Gnawing at my bottom lip, I explained, "I mean, I wasn't sure if we were just kickin' it as friends who happen to share a lime baby, *or...*"

"Or if I've really been this pressed to spend some time with you because I like you?" he interjected, his expression intense as he stared at me long and hard before slowly pulling me his way and meeting me in the middle for a kiss.

With his lips pressed against mine and every swirl of his tongue that followed, it felt like my question was being answered more and more thoroughly. But in case there was still any doubt on my part, Maverick pulled away just enough to confirm, "It's a date, Camryn."

That simple clarification set something off inside of me, almost like it had given me permission to do what I'd do if I was on a typical first date and it was going this well.

I kissed him again.

Except this time, it wasn't with the innocence of Maverick making his point. Nah, this kiss was with every bit of the extra hormones raging through me, turning me into a total animal once Maverick caught on and pulled me into his lap.

With his hands back under my sweatshirt, it was almost like I could feel an electric charge from every one of his fingertips as they slowly grazed my skin. And when he let them travel upwards only to discover I wasn't wearing a bra, something was set off for him too as he immediately pulled it over my head so that he could give my breasts some up-close attention.

"Be careful," I warned, knowing how tender they had been all day. But with Maverick's lips wrapped around my nipple, it didn't even matter, the pleasure from his perfect licks and suction making the pain from earlier irrelevant as I found myself completely caught up.

The longer he went back and forth between my nipples, the hotter I grew, desperate for anything that would bring me real relief since the friction from grinding against his erection wasn't doing nearly enough. And just when Maverick had me right at the brink of getting ready to beg for it, he lifted the both of us off of the couch so that he could carry me to the bedroom, kissing me up until the very last second when he gently deposited me onto the bed.

Taking a second to get out of his clothes, he teased, "Consider yourself lucky. I usually don't put out on the first date."

"Oh, wow. What an honor," I crooned, getting rid of my shorts and panties while playfully acknowledging, "First date dick from the person whose child I'm already carrying."

"Not just dick," he insisted with a smirk, slowly parting my legs before sliding face first between them. And with every swipe of his tongue against my clit, it felt like I was ascending towards the heavens, the extra sensitivity turning traditional foreplay into a divine experience that had me leaving huge wrinkles in the sheets after fisting them through my orgasm.

Of course, Maverick was only getting started, wiping his face on the comforter and then climbing up the bed to get to the main event. But before he could fill me up in a delicious fashion, I stopped him with a hand to his chest so that I could ask, "Do we need a condom?"

"Camryn, I think it's a little too late for condoms," he responded with a chuckle, adjusting his hovered position as I groaned, "Not for pregnancy purposes, *obviously*. I mean, are you having sex with anyone else?"

"Like who?"

"Like another woman, Mav," I answered, the fact that my original question hadn't exactly left room for confusion forcing me to brace myself for what must've been a complicated truth.

"Have I had sex with another woman since you? Yes. Have I had sex with anyone since learning about the baby? Absolutely not," he replied, bending his neck so that his face hovered right above mine when he added, "And I didn't want to. I've been waiting... for you."

Admittedly, I was worried that I might've ruined my own mood by bringing up other people. But after he said *that?*

I honestly couldn't get his dick inside of me fast enough, every inch making my body tingle as Maverick groaned, "Worth the wait." Then he followed it with this sloppy tongue kiss that, when combined with his slow strokes, had me ready to get pregnant all over again even though we were technically still in the first trimester.

It was just so damn... *intimate*. The kind of sex that if a baby was the result, you couldn't even be mad. But considering we were already *"been there, done that"*, I was free to enjoy it for what it was, free to embrace every bit of sensual energy oozing from Maverick when he asked, "You tryna make a nigga fall in love or somethin'? *Gotdamn*."

I could've echoed his sentiments since the dick he was giving up had me proud to be carrying his child like we'd done the shit on purpose, my eyes closed as he ramped up to a pace that had the headboard knocking and me screaming his praises.

"Yeah, Cam. Let Miss. Lady hear you. Let her know I'm hittin' it right," Maverick coached, my legs wrapped around his waist and my fingernails digging into his back as I breathily agreed, "*So right.*"

"Hm?" he grunted with a deep stroke that forced me to repeat myself a little louder.

"So right, baby!"

Against my ear, he groaned, "*Mm.* I like that shit. Call me that shit again."

"Right there, baby. *Yesss.* Right there," I screamed, my voice hoarse as Maverick gave me everything I was asking for and more. And just when I thought it couldn't get any better, he pulled out and took another trip downtown, the sensitivity from being so close to climaxing making me see stars as he licked and sucked my clit until I was begging him to get back inside of me.

When he finally listened, it came with a special request for me to ride him which was honestly music to my ears since controlling the pace meant I could get myself off faster and easily get him there too. But once I was on top, I found myself lost admiring Maverick, easily recognizing what had the girls going so crazy for him all around the world.

Maverick was fuckin' beautiful, and yet somehow still rugged. Cocky, but also had the ability to be a total sweetheart. A fuck-up on occasion, but at least he could admit it and apologize. And he cared about the people in his life immensely.

Truthfully, I was lucky to be in the number.

I was also lucky to feel his dick throbbing inside of me as

I came hard, collapsing against his chest as he let off without warning.

Grunting through this nut, he insisted, "If you weren't already pregnant, you definitely would be now."

"And if you weren't already going to be a father, *well…* congratulations," I told him playfully, climbing off of his dick to go clean myself up in the bathroom as he stayed in bed trying to gather the energy to do the same.

At least, that's what I thought he was doing until I returned to find him already asleep. And while it almost felt like an alternate universe for me to be so pleased by the sight of Maverick in my bed, I couldn't help the smile that came to my lips as I climbed back in and cuddled up against him.

MAVERICK

Waking up in Camryn's bed was already a big deal.

But waking up to Camryn kissing on my neck, clearly on a mission to wake *him* up too?

Yeah, that shit I couldn't have predicted on my luckiest day, a grin on my face as I cracked my eyes open just slightly and teased, "Damn, mamas. You ain't fuckin' around."

"Actually, that's exactly what I'm trying to do," she replied with a smirk, pinning my wrists over my head before asking, "You down?"

My erection alone should've been enough to answer her question. But in case there was any doubt, I gave an enthusiastic, "Hell yeah," watching her smirk turn even more giddy as she positioned herself *and...* her phone started buzzing.

Closing her eyes tightly, she groaned, "*Shit.* I gotta get that," already crawling off of my lap as I sat up on my elbows to ask, "It can't wait?"

"It's my mother," she answered,

"It can't wait," I repeated as a statement instead of a question, climbing out of the bed as I told her, "It's all good.

I gotta take a piss anyway. Keep that same energy when I get back, though. Aight?"

Giving a quick nod, she fluffed her hair before tapping the screen to answer the *Facetime* call with a super chipper, "Hi, Mommy. Good morning."

The rest of their conversation got drowned out once I made it to the bathroom where I took my time since I could pretty much assume Camryn wasn't about to rush her mother off the phone. Not to mention, peeing with a hard dick wasn't exactly the easiest to do.

Still, I got it done, got washed up, and made it back to the bedroom just in time to catch Camryn telling her mother, "Ummm... I have a busy few weeks at work coming up. But maybe I can drive up there for Father's Day?"

Taking a spot at the end of the bed - *out of the camera's view* - I heard her mother excitedly respond, "Oh, you know your daddy would love that. Let's make it a surprise."

Camryn's eyebrows shot up. "*A surprise.* Yeah. It will definitely be that."

Her reaction was suspicious to me. And apparently to her mother too according to the way she immediately asked, "You okay, Cammy Girl?"

"Yeah, everything's fine," Camryn answered airily. "I just... really miss you guys. Father's Day can't come soon enough."

"We miss you too, sweetheart," her mother crooned. "And you know you can come visit for stuff other than holidays, right?"

"I do. But with work and everything, it's just a lot going on."

Ahh, so that's what that reaction was about earlier.

The "A lot going on" that she still hadn't told her parents about.

Honestly, I couldn't even judge her since I hadn't told my mama either. Partially because I was nervous about what her reaction would be and partially to protect Camryn from being bombarded in any way. But it was ironic to hear Camryn's mother name drop when she replied, "Now you know I'm a huge Meredith Woods fan. But if that sister of hers is working you to death, I have no problem coming up there and whooping her..."

I was already laughing to myself as Camryn attempted to cut her mother off with a loud, "Whoa! *Hey*. Umm, I think I hear someone knocking at the door, so I should probably go see what's up. But we'll talk soon, okay? Love you, Mommy."

"Love you more, Cammy Girl," her mother sang sweetly before ending the call, Camryn immediately looking my way to say, "*Sorry*... about that."

"Don't apologize," I insisted, grabbing her foot so that I could massage it while telling her, "Mama bears make the best grandmas."

That made her smirk, taking a moment to enjoy my hands before asking, "I never did tell you good morning, huh?"

"Nah, too busy tryna get ya' freak on," I joked, tightening my grip on the foot she playfully tried to kick me with as I asked, "How you feelin', though? You aight?"

"Yeah, I'm good. You good?"

Nodding, I answered, "Better than good since I got to wake up to your pretty ass all over me."

Honestly, I would've thought it was a dream if she would've frowned and denied it. But instead, her smile remained as she acknowledged, "I see how you keep a girl around at all times. Your flattery game is truly undefeated."

"I'm being serious, though," I defended. "Last night was nice. Hopefully we can do it again soon."

Once the words left my lips, I realized how corny the shit probably sounded. But the truth was the truth. The night I'd spent with Camryn was something like my ideal Friday, the exact kind of thing I needed to balance out what my "work life" had become.

No cameras.

No noise.

No people.

Just me and my lady cozied up on the couch watching movies, enjoying each other's company and each other's bodies with the baby monitor nearby.

Obviously, the baby monitor would be a future addition. And technically, Camryn being my lady was something for the future too. But the other stuff we could do sooner than later, Camryn leaning towards the former when she asked, "Well... what do you have going on today?"

"I gotta work later on tonight, but that's about it."

With a inquisitive look, she questioned, "Work, as in, make an appearance at a party?"

Moving up the bed a little bit, I slipped my hand under her shirt so that I could rub her stomach while answering, "Yeah, papa has to make some money before his baby girl gets here to spend it all."

Of course, we still had a few weeks before we'd officially find out the baby's gender. But something told me God was about to bless me with a princess to spoil rotten. A mini version of her mother with the same mocha brown skin and curly hair, and a mini version of me with an affinity for designer wear and exclusive sneakers.

I was already thinking about what kicks I'd start her collection off with when Camryn inquired, "How much *do* you make from that? Not that I'm trying to clock your pockets, I'm just curious."

"For something like tonight that's local? I'll probably make about fifteen racks," I answered with a shrug, knowing I was really doing the promoter a favor by giving him a rate on the lower end of my appearance fee. But considering I didn't have to travel anywhere and probably would've gone out anyway to hear my boy Whoa spin since I'd missed him the last time he was DJing, it wasn't that big of a deal.

Well... it wasn't that big of a deal to *me.*

Camryn, on the other hand, damn near hopped off the bed when she asked, "Just for showing up to one party?! That's insane! Where do I sign up?"

Chuckling, I answered, "You can roll with me tonight if you want. I mean, you wouldn't get paid. But you'd at least get to see what it's like and maybe even get some leverage for when you wanna do your own thing."

I was honestly a little excited about the prospect of putting Camryn on until she giggled, "That was a joke, Mav. One, I can't drink, so a party at a club is an automatic no-go. Two, I enjoy my privacy way too much to be seen out in public with you right now."

For as much as I could understand her desire to remain lowkey, the truth was, "You can't hide forever, Camryn."

It was almost inevitable that once she started showing, the public would pick up on some random clue that connected the two of us and a whole bunch of unwanted attention would come her way. Still, Camryn remained convinced that she could continue to fly under the radar the entire time, a confident smirk on her lips when she replied, "Challenge accepted, Maverick."

Instead of trying to change her mind, I changed the subject, thinking back on the conversation I'd walked in on when I asked, "So your parents want you to come visit, huh?"

"Yeah. I really can't hide forever in that regard," she answered with a heavy sigh that told me just how much the thought of facing them was already weighing on her. But to me, that wasn't something she should have to bear alone which was why I offered, "Want me to come with you? For back up?"

Like I'd said something wild, her eyes went wide in surprise. "You'd do that?"

"Of course, Camryn," I answered with a bit of a laugh. "Why you sound so shocked?"

"I mean, meeting the parents is kinda a big deal."

"Having a child together is an even bigger deal," I countered. "And I'm sure your parents are gonna wanna meet the man who's gone half wit' you after you break the news. What better time than Father's Day to announce who's the father?"

Squinting, she cocked her head and insisted, "I see the vision, but I don't think it works like that."

"Father's Day, but you're actually gonna be a grandfather?" I suggested, watching her smirk as she replied, "Better, but still not quite it."

Using my version of her voice, I made another attempt. "Hey Dad, this is Maverick. He's gonna be a dad soon too… of my child."

Laughing hard, she finally climbed out of the bed while telling me, "I appreciate the effort, but that is quite literally the worst introduction I've ever heard."

"Good thing we got all day to come up with a better one, huh?" I reminded her, pulling her backwards and down into my lap the second she started to pass me.

It was almost like I couldn't stop touching her, couldn't

get enough of having her close. And I was glad she didn't seem to mind, settling deeper into my embrace as she asked over her shoulder, "Oh, do we now?"

"Yeah, I was thinking I could go and grab us some breakfast right quick. Maybe rewatch the movie, get reinspired..." I trailed right against her ear, making her giggle as she vowed, "If we're rewatching the movie, it's gonna get my undivided attention this time."

"You wanna bet?" I challenged, slipping my hand into her panties as proof that she was up against stiff competition.

I mean, *really* stiff competition that was already reacting to the discovery of how wet Camryn was when she opened herself a little wider to give me better access to her pussy. And now I felt like I had no choice but to make her cum; no choice but to give her what she was after when I woke up to her on top of me even as she moaned my name in defiance.

"I meant it when I told you to keep that same energy, Camryn," I scolded, playing with her clit as she moaned, "I knowww. But now that you brought up breakfast..."

"You tellin' me I can't have you for breakfast, Cammy Girl?" I teased, the use of her nickname making her giggle through her moans before she physically removed my hand so that she could answer, "I really need to eat somethin' first."

"Only because that means my baby gets to eat too will I let you slide," I decided, letting her up before moving from the bed to get the rest of my clothes on. "Now what y'all want to eat?"

"*Ummm...* I can probably just make us something," she suggested, her response stopping me in my tracks since... "You're gonna cook for me?"

I knew women never cooked for guys they didn't really

like. But of course, she still tried to make it sound like nothing when she replied, "It's only breakfast, Mav."

"Yeah, breakfast after spending the night, spending the night *after...*"

"*Anyway*," she interrupted. "You need a toothbrush or anything?"

"Nah, I have one in my bag in the car," I told her, getting ready to put my shoes on so that I could go and grab it until I saw the way she was staring at me.

"*Wait*. You brought an overnight bag with you? So you knew this was going to happen?"

To be honest, I was never a thousand percent sure of anything when it came to Camryn. But I also didn't want to end up in a situation where I psyched myself out so much that I was unprepared for the best-case scenario of earning more of her time, feeling proud about how things had played out when I finally answered, "Stay ready so you ain't gotta get ready, Cammy Girl. I'll be right back."

Shaking her head with a smile, she sent me on my way. And I would've been lying if I didn't admit to the extra pep in my step as I hit the hallway, totally missing the fact that Camryn's neighbor was standing in her doorway until she said, "Morning, Nate. Great performance last night. I don't think I've ever heard her get that loud."

On one hand, I was trippin' off the fact that she really called herself rating my sex game, lowkey grossed out that she'd even made a point to listen in. But on the other hand, I was glad to hear I was an upgrade in comparison to whatever Camryn used to put up with, a polite grin on my face when I responded, "Good to know."

Since I kept walking, I figured that'd be the end of it until she pressed, "So what's the secret? Or would you rather just come in and demonstrate?"

Her suggestion made me laugh as I turned around to answer, "Tempting offer, Miss. Lady. But that's a special young woman you have for a neighbor, and I'll be damned if I let another, equally special young woman come between us."

"*Young?*" she repeated with a frown. "Boy, you better put some respect on my age. I've only gotten better with time. These old negros just can't keep up. Or keep *it* up."

"*Way more than I needed to know,*" I thought, doing my best to keep things cordial when I tossed a hand towards the door and told her, "I uh... gotta go grab somethin' from the car. But you have yourself a good Saturday, aight?"

"You too, Nate."

"Maverick," I corrected. "Nate's my... middle name."

Obviously, that wasn't true either. But I figured it was the easiest way to rectify things without sounding like a total fraud; though it still resulted in a frown from Miss. Lady once she asked, "Why the hell would you go by your middle name with a first name as powerful as Maverick?"

"It's a... weird family tradition," I lied. "You can call me Maverick from now on, though."

"Alright now, *Maverick.* Looking good, *Maverick.* See you later, *Maverick,*" she replied like she had to rehearse it a few times to get used to it. But I'd let her say my real name a million times if that meant not having to play Nate anymore, glad to have another problem solved as my phone started to buzz just as I got to the car.

Popping the trunk, I pressed the phone to my ear and answered, "Morning, Mali."

"Hey, Mav. What you doin'?"

"About to have breakfast with the mother of my child. What's up?"

"Breakfast, huh? That's cute," she cooed, making me

roll my eyes as she got to the real point of her phone call. "Anyway, I wanted to see if I could be your plus one tonight? For that party you're making an appearance at?"

"Since when do you wanna roll with me to my gigs?" I asked, finding it a little suspicious even when she defended, "I can't hang out with my brother now?"

Chuckling, I clarified, "I didn't say that. But you've never really cared to join me for somethin' like this, so what's the deal?"

Releasing a little sigh, she admitted, "I *just...* could really use a night out. And I figured the one with family and free liquor would be my best option."

Something told me that wasn't the full story. But it still sounded reasonable enough for me to agree, "Fine, Mali. Meet me at my place at eleven."

"Thank youuuu," she sang, ending the call with a giddy, "See you tonight." And while I still found the whole thing strange, I figured it could be dealt with later on since right now was about making the most of my time with Camryn.

I should've never left Camryn's apartment.

After spending the day with her, kicking it hard and eating everything - *and I do mean everything* - in sight, being in the club for two contractually-obligated hours was really starting to feel like a job, forcing me to dig deep and find the energy to periodically socialize so the promoter wouldn't think I was intentionally trying to be standoffish.

It didn't help that my sister had straight up played my ass, making it sound like her joining me was for some much-needed relaxation and bonding when she was really just using me to get to somebody else who she knew would be in attendance. And while I couldn't exactly knock her game, it was still annoying to have to entertain a bunch of strangers when I could've just spent the two hours pretending to have fun with her.

Nah, Malinda was actually a really good time whenever we did end up in the same places. But tonight, her attention was elsewhere meaning I was splitting my time between the crowd and my phone.

Sipping from my drink, I used my other hand to scroll through my album of recent photos, smiling at the ones I'd taken of myself and Camryn this afternoon while she was napping on my chest. And just as I was starting to imagine what it would be like doing the same thing with our baby in the mix, a familiar voice knocked me out of my dream.

"We gettin' tacos after this?"

Peeking up from my phone, I saw Sophia standing there looking club-ready with a smirk on her face, the fact that she had my attention prompting her to step even closer to say, "It's been a minute, Mav."

"Little bit," I agreed, sipping from my drink as my eyes went back to the crowd since I knew that wouldn't get me in trouble. But of course, that didn't stop Sophia from trying me anyway, moving an inch closer to ask, "You're not gonna offer me a drink? I thought we were better than that, babe?"

The hint of alcohol on her breath as she spoke told me she'd already had her fair share of liquor. But again, since I wasn't trying to have any trouble, I told her, "We good, Soph. It's a bottle over there on ice. Help yourself."

"Or *maybe*, I can just have a sip of yours," she insisted, pulling the glass out of my hand for much more than a sip before attempting to hand it back to me.

"Keep it," I insisted, getting ready to head back into the

crowd until she caught me by the arm to confess, "I miss you, Mav."

Considering we hadn't even spoken to each other since the day she blew up on me, *the day I found out about the baby*, it was ironic to hear her say that now that we were face-to-face. But I suppose it wouldn't have mattered if she'd said that shit the very next day since all of my attention had been with Camryn anyway, something I was getting ready to share with Sophia until she pulled me closer to ask, "Come home with me tonight."

No lie, Sophia wasn't making shit any easier for me. I mean, she was an attractive woman, and we'd always had fire chemistry. But when I thought about everything I'd be risking by entertaining her even a little bit, the decision was easy, the confident smirk on my lips giving her false hope when I answered, "Nah. I'm good," pulling away with a casual, "You be well, though."

Obviously, she wasn't happy about that. But she knew better than to cause a real scene. And while I was glad to have survived the close call, I knew I didn't want to leave myself vulnerable for any other run-ins, glad to see the clock working in my favor as I checked my phone while approaching my sister who was hanging by the DJ booth.

Tapping her on the shoulder to get her attention, I leaned in near her ear to ask, "Mali, you about ready to dip?"

Frowning, she moved towards my ear to respond, "I thought you said you had to stay 'til 1:30?"

"On the dot," I told her, lifting my phone into view to show her the clock as proof that my job was indeed finished.

Still, that wasn't enough to keep my sister from growing suspicious, her expression skeptical when she yelled over the music, "Maverick, is everything alright?"

Nodding, I moved back to her ear to answer, "Yeah, I'm just not really feelin' this shit tonight." And after catching her understanding nod in response, I continued, "But if you wanna stick around, you can. Just make sure Whoa gets you home safely."

Pulling her face away to find my eyes, she yelled, "Why would Walter be responsible for making sure I get home?"

"Mali, you ain't foolin' nobody," I told her with a smirk, moving past her to show my boy Whoa some love with a quick dap before pulling my sister into a hug where I advised, "Text me when you make it to... wherever your final destination ends up being."

"Goodnight, asshole," she giggled with a little shove to my arm that sent me on my way. And I was glad that I was in position to make a clean exit out of the back instead of having to deal with the crowd, the exhaustion from just those two hours hitting me the second I climbed into the private car I was glad I'd splurged on for the night.

The ride home wasn't long enough for me to get any real sleep. But it was the perfect amount of time for me to go back to the pictures I'd been looking at earlier, lowkey tempted to hit Camryn up and see if she was awake enough to let me into her place.

Okay, actually I was more than tempted, quickly deciding it was worth a shot when I sent her a text.

"You still up, mamas?" - Maverick

If nothing else, she'd respond in the morning. And by the time I got home, got changed, and got to bed, I figured that would be the case, taking my ass to sleep only to wake up to a text from her that was not exactly the kind of energy I was expecting.

"Let me guess. Not what it looks like?" - Camryn

I had no idea what she was talking about until I clicked the link that was attached to her message, directing me to an *Instagram* post that had a picture of Sophia and I appearing to be in the middle of an intimate conversation and a ridiculous ass lie of a caption.

"#LoveTriangleAlert Now we THOUGHT Maverick Woods and Lillian Banks were back together. But as y'all can see, he was spotted in the club last night getting cozy with his in-between thing, Sophia. Is she just keeping him occupied until Lillian gets out of rehab, or are we witnessing a full-blown love triangle? Let us know what you think in the comments!"

Without even looking at the comments, I already knew they were a total disaster. So instead of wasting any time with them, I went back to the text thread so that I could respond to Camryn.

"Not even close. Shit is crazy. I'm so sorry, Cam. For real." - Maverick

I could only imagine how that picture made her feel, especially after the amazing night and day we'd spent together. And while I knew I didn't have any control over whatever the bloggers made up, I still felt it was necessary to apologize for even letting that shit be speculated from my actions; something that Camryn also alluded to in her response.

"Don't be sorry, Mav. Be more careful." - Camryn

"Everything just happened so fast." - Maverick

"And as you very well know, the cameras happen even faster." - Camryn

"Fuckin' facts," I said out loud, more mad at myself than anything for not nipping that shit in the bud right away. But now that it was already out there, the most I could do was stick to the truth and plead my case.

"It wasn't anything, I swear. I hope you believe me." - Maverick

"It's not about me believing you or not. It's about you not ending up in these situations in the first place." - Camryn

"I thought I had it handled and she caught me off-guard. But I promise you, it won't happen again." - Maverick

Considering this wasn't exactly the first time we'd dealt with something like this, I couldn't even be mad if she didn't receive my words favorably. But it was all I had until I was given another chance to prove myself, something that Camryn didn't seem very thrilled about according to her dry reply of, **"Yeah, we'll see."**

CAMRYN

The baby had officially bumped.

Maybe not to the public eye. But I could definitely see a little something as I went back and forth between my front view and side view in the mirror, the roundness in my lower abdomen making me giddy and teary all at once since it only solidified what I was still coming to terms with.

I was really about to be somebody's mom.

It might've sounded ridiculous. But in many ways, even being a solid fourteen weeks into this thing, I was still in shock. Especially since I was actively going through the motions of my life like nothing had changed.

Work was still work.

Home was still home.

The in-between stuff was still the in-between stuff.

The only difference was there was another life growing inside of me that, being completely honest, it was almost easy to forget about sometimes now that my morning sickness had calmed.

Keyword: sometimes.

With every day that past, I still knew I was an inch closer to the finish line. And now that I could see the baby beyond the ultrasound, that fact only became more real.

I was really about to be somebody's mom.

Releasing a heavy sigh, I started rehearsing the different ways I could break the news to my own mama in my head only to be interrupted by a phone call from Andria, a welcomed distraction even when she joked, "Hey, Camryn Carebear Cox. What you doin'?"

Tucking the phone between my ear and shoulder, I headed to my closet and answered, "Just getting all packed up so that I can hit the road first thing in the morning."

"Oh, that trip to your parents' is this weekend, huh?"

"Sure is," I replied as I sorted through my clothes for the perfect Father's Day/Announcement Day dress, quickly deciding on something loose and flowy just in case I chickened out. But the idea of chickening out almost felt impossible once Andria asked, "Is Maverick still going with you?"

"Umm... I'm not really sure. We haven't talked about it," I answered honestly.

I mean, of course he knew the trip was happening. And yes, we'd talked about him joining me when it was first brought up. But after the internet shit a few weeks back, things hadn't been as chill and organic between us as they once were, almost like we were back to square one... *again.*

Even though I didn't necessarily like it, it seemed like the safest way to keep myself from getting hurt since having my feelings in Maverick's hand was just a dangerous game to play.

Not that I thought he was intentionally out to do something foul. But with everything that had already happened, it was almost like he couldn't help attracting nonsense. And considering there were a million other things for me to be focusing on right now, putting energy towards sorting through Maverick's drama just didn't seem worth the effort.

Of course, Andria saw it differently, making it seem ridiculous that I hadn't confirmed Maverick's attendance when she asked, "Why haven't y'all talked about it?"

"I don't know. I've just been busy," I told her, pulling a couple dress options to pack as Andria pressed, "Busy trying to decide if you can really trust him or not?"

It was almost like she'd read my mind, easily pinning down the true reason why I was trying to avoid this altogether. But now that it was out, I could only plop down on the bed with another sigh before asking, "Am I wrong for questioning that?"

"Not at all. But you also can't just continue to avoid him *and* your own feelings. I mean, regardless of what Mav has going on, y'all are still having a baby together."

The mention of the baby reminded me to share, "He sent flowers to my job the other day. Thank you flowers."

"Thank you for that ass flowers?"

"No, thank you for the baby flowers," I giggled, quickly realizing, "So I guess, kinda for that ass?"

Either way, it was an obvious effort on his part to get us back on track. And you would've thought Andria was working for his campaign the way she asked, "Outside of a couple questionable photos, has he really given you a reason not to trust him? I mean, it's not like his explanations haven't made any sense."

That was what made all of this even more difficult.

Everything made so much sense. I knew how things worked with him being in the spotlight. And yet, it still didn't sit quite right with me, a feeling that had me torn as I told Andria, "I know. I *just*... how do I know this isn't Nate all over again? You know, me just going along with whatever he says and pretending like it makes me feel better when it doesn't?"

Don't get me wrong, I appreciated Maverick's honesty. But just because it wasn't what it seemed didn't mean I wasn't affected by the slew of people speaking life into the lies, dissecting every detail, making a whole bunch of something out of what one person - *the person involved* - claimed was nothing. It was easy to say ignore the comments, focus on "real life", fuck social media altogether. But that didn't stop it from existing, and it damn sure didn't stop me from potentially being affected, especially considering how big of a role social media played in Maverick's life.

It was what kept him popular enough to do club appearances. His following was what allowed him to make four and five figures from a simple sponsored post. And the stuff he shared in between was what kept his fans - *mostly women* - happy and engaged.

So how was it even possible for everything he did on social media to be so purposeful, and yet I was still supposed to pretend like social media wasn't all that important?

The complicated nature of it all was exactly why I'd been trying to avoid the Maverick circus in the first place. But now, here I was, the elephant balancing on the barrel who was struggling to roll myself to the other stool.

Or rather, roll myself to the end of this pregnancy.

The analogy had me sad for both myself and the real-life circus animals as Andria said, "You have every right to feel however you choose to. But Maverick isn't Nate, Camryn. People literally get paid to catch him slippin' even when he's not, meaning it's really not all that farfetched to give him the benefit of the doubt."

Frowning, I asked, "Who would've thought you'd be on #TeamMaverick with this?"

"What can I say? Real recognize real," she insisted, surely giving a little shrug as she continued, "Seriously, though. If nothing else, Maverick has been especially supportive when it comes to everything you and the baby. I can't imagine him not wanting to support you through this too."

"No, you're right," I agreed with a nod she couldn't see. "I guess I just have to stop overthinking it."

Even with everything else Maverick had going on, he still deserved the opportunity to be a part of this moment; deserved to be able to stand up for himself in front of my parents and make his commitment to their grandchild clear. And not only that, I kinda wanted him there; maybe even needed him there to really believe I'd be good no matter how they reacted.

If nothing else, I knew he'd have my back regardless.

Like she was responding to my inner thoughts and my earlier realization, Andria replied, "*Exactly*. Now let me get off your line so you can call your baby daddy and make sure he knows the plan for tomorrow."

Giggling, I told her goodbye and ended the call so that I could do exactly what she'd said.

Well... almost exactly, opting for a text instead of a call just in case he was out and about.

"Hey. You still free to tag-a-long this weekend?" - Camryn

"What you mean, tag-a-long? The playlist is made, the snacks are bought, and the gas tank on the G-Wagon is already full.

Honestly, if anybody is tagging along, it's you." - Maverick

Wait a minute...

"I'm tagging along to my own parents' house?" - Camryn

"Already got the blanket in the passenger seat for you, mamas. All you gotta do is ride and relax." - Maverick

The fact that he was so prepared and had now volunteered to drive relieved some stress I didn't even know I was carrying, a smile on my face as I typed out a curious response.

"And I was supposed to know all of this how?" - Camryn

"You thought I was going to leave you hanging? I told you I was coming, and I'm a man of my word." - Maverick

If Maverick Woods would've said that same phrase to me months ago, I would've literally laughed in his face. But as of late, I'd been witnessing a different side of him that made it hard for me downplay its truth.

Maverick was changing, *growing*, maturing in ways I didn't even know was possible. And truthfully, I was glad to be on the receiving end, feeling good about it when I replied, **"Well in that case, I guess I'll see you in the morning."**

Maverick was not at all lying about how prepared he was.

He had way more snacks than necessary for a three-hour drive. He had an assortment of playlists curated for whatever vibe I was feeling. He had a heated blanket for me to get some rest under, and he even had gifts for my parents - a nice bottle of red wine for my mom and something equivalent in scotch for my dad.

They were going to love his ass. And really, with all his thoughtfulness, he was making himself hard not to love; even for someone like me who thought for certain he was the worst. But really, that was a me problem, putting so much stock into his online persona that I never gave much thought to how he operated with those he really cared about outside of his immediate family.

Now I knew better.

In everything he did, it was obvious how much he cared about me and the baby. And while I still wasn't sure if that translated to us being in an actual relationship, the fact that he was only the second man I'd be introducing to my parents meant something.

Sure, the circumstances weren't ideal. But I wasn't exactly cringing at the thought of them all becoming acquainted. In fact, I was actually excited to see what they thought of Maverick, realizing I'd be learning soon enough once we pulled into my parents' driveway.

"I can't even fake. This is almost exactly what I envisioned your childhood home to look like," Maverick mentioned as he pulled our bags out of the trunk, the short trip to the front porch giving me a chance to ask, "Modest and comfortable?"

"Warm and inviting," he clarified, a fair description for the very traditional two-story home my parents had worked their asses off to afford back in their early twenties.

I could still remember when we first moved here, could remember how excited I was to have my own room and a backyard. And of course, I could remember all the pictures that had been taken on the front porch we were standing on as I started to press the doorbell until I saw the front door already being opened.

Instead of acknowledging me, my mother's eyes went straight to Maverick as she leaned against the doorframe to flirt, "What *exactly* can I do for you, young man?"

"Mommy!" I squealed embarrassedly as she stepped out onto the porch to pull me into a hug.

"Oh, hey Cammy Girl. *Sorry.* I was just a little distracted," she mentioned like I hadn't noticed. "It's so good to see you, baby. Now who is your friend?"

"Mommy, this is Maverick," I told her, reversing the introduction when I said, "Maverick, this is my mother."

Extending his arms for a hug, Maverick announced, "Very nice to meet you, Mrs. Cox. Easy to see where Camryn gets her good looks from."

"Oh, honey. Call me Cindy," my mother insisted with a giggle as she accepted his embrace. "And I don't know who you get your good looks from, but *chile...*"

Before she could get too ahead of herself, I interjected, "Mommy, this is Ms. Meredith's son."

"Meredith Woods?" she asked, glancing at Maverick and then back at me to say, "Cammy Girl, you didn't tell me you were bringing black Hollywood royalty home with you."

That made Maverick chuckle as he bashfully replied, "Nah, I'm just lucky to be the offspring of greatness."

Of course, my mother ate that right up, grinning hard as my father approached the front door asking, "Cindy, who is that you're out there talk... Cammy Girl!"

Blowing past my mother, my father gave me the warm welcome I was expecting, his tight embrace bringing me to tears as I happily told him, "Hi, Daddy! Happy Almost Father's Day."

I realized I wasn't the only one who'd gotten emotional once my father pulled away so that he could wipe his own eyes, the sight making the reunion even more special when he said, "I didn't know you were coming to town."

"It was a surprise," my mother shared proudly now that we'd successfully pulled it off, the two of us sharing a celebratory smile as my father wiped the last of his tears.

"Well as y'all can see, y'all got me good," my father chuckled, doing his best to pull himself back together so that he could ask, "Now who is this little nigga you got on my porch lookin' like a damn Sean John ad?"

"Daddy, be nice," I scolded with a giggle as Mav extended his hand to introduce himself.

"Maverick Woods. It's good to meet you, sir."

Instinctively, my father remained skeptical until my mother tagged on, "Maverick is the son of Meredith Woods."

"Fine ah... *I mean*, the wonderfully *talented* actress Meredith Woods?" my father asked, watching all three of us nod before he said, "Still doesn't explain what you're doin' on my porch."

Like it wasn't obvious, I explained, "He's here with me, Daddy. We came together."

I figured that would at least be enough to get us inside until my father pressed, "This your boyfriend now?

"*Uh…*"

"Yeah, I am," Maverick answered confidently, tossing an arm over my shoulder to add, "And I'm also going *to…*"

"Hand over the gift he was so thoughtful to pick up for the both of you," I interrupted nervously, Maverick peeking my way confusedly like he wasn't wrong for almost outing us without any sort of warm-up.

Thankfully, all it took was a pleading look for him to follow my lead by reaching into his bag to hand over the bottles he'd gotten for each of them, my father glancing at his to say, "Blue Label Johnnie Walker? Should've led with that, nigga."

"Just say thank you, Teddy," my mother scolded, making up for my father's poor manners when she cheerfully responded, "That was so nice of you, Maverick. This wine will go great with dinner. Now you two go on upstairs and get settled in right quick so we can eat."

Making our way inside, Maverick once again followed my lead when he carried our bags upstairs to my childhood bedroom. But the second we were cleared for some privacy, I got in his ass, speaking as quietly yet aggressively as I could when I asked, "Maverick, what the fuck was that?"

"*What?* I figured it'd be best if we just came right out with it. You know, yank the band-aid off."

While it was clear just how much sense it made in his head, the fact that he'd almost sent me into a full-blown panic attack had me upset enough to groan, "You can come right out with it to your own mother, Mav. This, *with them*, is for me to do."

Nodding, he agreed, "You right. My bad," the acknowledgment of his wrongdoing still not quite enough to put me at ease until he pulled me into a hug and advised, "Just relax, mamas. It's gonna be fine. I'm here."

I wanted to believe him. But after that close call earlier, I wasn't as confident as I had been, feeling every bit of nervous as we finally headed back downstairs where I was greeted with a glass of wine from my mother.

"Here, Cammy Girl. Try this. It's delicious."

In the blink of an eye, the glass was already in my hand. And while I probably could've gotten away with a sip or two without hurting my baby, I still couldn't bring myself to do it, trying not to make it obvious as I sat the glass down on the counter with a casual, "Actually, I'm good for now."

"Told you," my father chirped from the sidelines, my expression turning confused as I asked, "Told her what?" And my heart only started beating even faster when I noticed, "Mommy, why are you crying?"

"I'm just so happy for you, baby," she sang, already pulling me into a hug as my father explained, "The boyfriend we ain't never heard about 'til now and the unexplainable glow? Turning down good wine? Your ass is pregnant, ain't you?"

Considering how far along I was, denying it would've been dumb. And while this obviously wasn't the way I expected it to go, now that they'd already pieced things together on their own, I really had no choice but to answer, "Yeah, I am. Fourteen weeks."

There was this moment of silence as my parents first looked at each other, then looked at me, and finally looked at Maverick who was standing nearby wide-eyed like a deer in headlights. And as my father approached him, I don't think any of us knew what to expect, Daddy taking a moment to size him up before his lips finally curled upwards into a grin.

"Congratulations, big dog," he told Mav, dapping him up and pulling him into a hug that relieved us all as my mother whined, "Cammy Girl, I can't believe you've been hiding this from meee. No wonder you haven't been wanting to visit. You knew we would've sniffed you out right away."

Considering how things had played out, and that my plan had really been to tell them tomorrow, I could only chuckle as I replied, "Clearly I still underestimated your abilities."

Making a quick exchange, my mother moved to congratulate Maverick while my father gave me another tight hug. "Happy for you, Cammy Girl. Even though I'm way too young and handsome to be somebody's pop-pop."

Giggling, I reminded him, "You were also too young to be somebody's Daddy, but here you are anyway."

With a quick glance down at me and then further down to my belly, he agreed, "I guess I did aight."

"Daddy!"

"I'm just sayin'," he chuckled, looking back at Mav to say, "I hope y'all got some plans."

"Don't worry, sir. Your daughter is in good hands," Maverick assured him, shooting me a wink that made me blush as we finally settled in for dinner.

Of course with the announcement of the baby, my mother had a million questions about my pregnancy so far. My father, on the other hand, had a million questions for Maverick regarding what he actually did for a living and how he planned to provide for the baby and me.

Most of it I knew, but some was news to me, like his

plans to load up on all of his work travel now so that he could be fully present for the baby's first few months. And how he'd already sold off some of his exclusive sneakers to both start the baby's college fund and make more room in his apartment. And how he was thinking of rebranding as a "fashionable dad influencer", something my father didn't really understand even though I could very clearly see the vision.

Long story short, I was impressed, and excited, and... *maybe* even a bit turned on as I listened to Maverick speak on the future he saw for himself and for our baby. But when my dad pressed him specifically about what future he saw with me, I lowkey wanted to crawl under the table, not at all expecting Maverick to grab my hand when he very confidently replied, "Camryn's it for me."

My mother gave an exaggerated, "Awww" as I stared at Maverick long and hard, waiting for him to give me the cue that he was really just trying to sell us as a thing. But that wasn't the case. He was deadass serious. And being completely honest, I didn't know how to react since I'd never been in a situation like this.

Obviously, with a baby involved, things were much different than anything I'd ever experienced. But even beyond that, I'd never had someone be so sure about wanting to be with me, had never heard someone sound so confident about a future together.

I didn't want to get so wrapped up in the moment that I forgot about everything in the outside world that we still had to deal with, or forgot about the uncertain terms we'd come here on. But I also didn't want to ignore what was staring me right in the face, the fact that Maverick really wanted this; really wanted us.

To get us through the moment, I gave a smile that led

into more conversation about my upcoming birthday and their plans to visit. Then we finished up with dessert and the liquor that I couldn't indulge in but still felt good watching my parents and *my...* boyfriend enjoy together.

By the end of the night, I was happily exhausted. Excited to spend more time with my folks the next day, but even more excited to go to sleep; especially since being in bed came with its own privilege of having Maverick cuddled up behind me.

My grin was irremovable when I told him, "Well that certainly went a lot better than I thought it would."

"I really don't see why you were ever trippin'. Your parents are cool as fuck," he replied, gently kissing my shoulder as I nodded to agree.

"Yeah, it's honestly amazing to think they had me as high schoolers and are still happily together all these years later."

"Ahh, so the "oops" baby thing runs in the family, huh?" he asked teasingly, earning himself a little heel kick to the shin as I groaned, "Shut up, Mav."

"I mean, I get it, though. Y'all Cox women are *irresistibly* fine," he groaned with another kiss to my shoulder, letting this one trail towards my neck where I moaned, "*Mmm...* you better stop."

"And you better keep quiet," he replied as he slipped under the covers, the way he slowly moved about against the full-sized mattress like he was really trying to be sneaky making me giggle until I felt his mouth on my clit.

Just like that, my giggles were turned to moans as Maverick stretched my panties to the limit so that he could have full access to my pussy. And considering how much the man loved to satisfy me with his mouth, I honestly wasn't sure how he expected me to keep quiet; especially once he added his fingers to the mix.

With two gliding in and out of me and his tongue teasing my clit, it was damn near impossible not to make a little noise. And while the pillow over my face was the only thing saving me, it quickly became useless once Maverick decided it was dick 'o clock.

Pulling the pillow away, he tossed it out of my reach with a demand for me to turn over. And I did, *happily*, propping myself up on all fours as Maverick entered me from behind with a slow stroke that had me biting so hard into my bottom lip I thought for sure I was going to break the skin. But once we found a rhythm that kept the headboard quiet and the both of us satisfied, I felt like I could've spent the rest of the night just like that, Maverick's hands resting against my waist as he filled me over and over again until I came with a full body shudder.

Not being able to outwardly moan my way through the waves definitely made it hit harder. And with Maverick finding just the right spot to get himself there too, I couldn't help but grin as he came inside of me in long, gratifying spurts.

"By far the best dick I've ever gotten in this room," I told him as he pulled out, guiding me to lay on my side as he collapsed in front of me with a playful frown on his face.

"Considering you probably haven't fucked anyone in here as an adult, I'm struggling to take that as a compliment."

"Fair," I giggled. "But you still rewrote history. Be proud of that, baby."

Shaking his head with a smirk, he pulled me against his chest, gently running his fingers up and down my back as he mentioned, "I'm mad you ain't tell me you had a birthday comin' up next month."

"If you really knew me, you'd know," I defended, Maverick immediately sucking his teeth before asking, "Aight, so when's my birthday then?"

"January 19th," I answered to his surprise according to the way he sat up a little bit to ask, "How you know that?"

"Your form at the doctor," I explained, tilting my head back to find his eyes when I added, "I also know you're allergic to peanuts."

"Only mildly," he insisted. "But this ain't about me. This is about you and your birthday on…"

"July 22nd," I finished for him, the calendar in Maverick's head allowing him to conclude, "A weekday. So we'll do somethin' light on the actual day, and then we'll turn up on the weekend when your parents come to town."

It sounded good, but I still couldn't help asking, "So now you're in charge of my birthday plans?"

"In charge of making sure you have the best birthday ever? Yeah, I don't think it's all that unusual for your boyfriend to handle that."

My boyfriend.

I was well aware that this trip had the potential to be life-changing in a number of ways, but I certainly wasn't expecting that to include Maverick referring to himself as my boyfriend. And while I knew there was still a lot for us to conquer back home, for now I was going to soak up every bit of peace that came with him temporarily being out of the spotlight.

MAVERICK

Now I knew why Camryn didn't go to the movies often.

For her actual birthday, I'd rented out a single theater for us to privately enjoy some animated movie she claimed she wanted to see. But we weren't even twenty minutes into the flick when I caught her ass snoring, her half-emptied popcorn resting against her baby bump and what was left of her Icee melting in the cupholder nearby as I shook my head with a grin.

"Happy Birthday, mamas," I whispered, leaning over to deliver a gentle kiss to her cheek that unintentionally caused her to stir. And once she realized what was going on, she was quick to straighten up in her seat and give an unnecessary apology.

"I'm sorry. You didn't spend all this money just for me to be in here sleep."

"Actually, I spent a little bit of money for us to be able to do whatever the fuck we wanted in here," I corrected, understanding that rest was high on the priority list now that Camryn was almost halfway through the second trimester;

though her head was apparently on some other shit according to the way she smirked when insisting, "Don't get any ideas."

"I wasn't even talkin' about that, nasty," I chuckled. "But shit, now that you got it in my head..."

Before I could get too ahead of myself, she interjected, "Thank you, Maverick. This was really sweet of you."

"We're just gettin' started, mamas. Only the best for my girls," I told her as I lifted the armrest between us so that I could pull her closer, Camryn adjusting herself under my arm before peeking up to ask, "You're really trying to speak this baby girl thing into existence for next week's appointment, huh?"

Shaking my head, I answered, "Nah, I don't have to speak it cause I already know what's up."

Sure, there was no scientific reason for me to be so confident. But ever since finding out about the baby, I hadn't envisioned it going any other way. Not that I'd be disappointed if it was a boy. Honestly, I'd be geeked either way. But something about this one just felt like a girl, *my princess*, being carried by the queen who gave a little yawn before snuggling up closer against me to watch the rest of the movie.

How much of it she actually caught, I wasn't sure. But by the time the credits started to roll, she was still tired enough to groan, "I should've taken the rest of the week off."

"Already taken care of," I told her, catching the surprised look on her face as I went on to explain, "Auntie J agreed that you were more than deserving of some extra time away from work."

Really, I'd campaigned for Camryn's time off so that I could surprise her with a couple days of pampering before

Saturday's big event. But even without knowing any of that, she was still excited enough to wrap herself around my arm for the walk to the car that we both threw our hoods on for.

"*Wow*. You really are the king of gift-giving."

"I am, huh?" I asked playfully, planting a kiss to her forehead before helping her into the passenger seat. Then I made my way to the driver's side, reaching into the backseat to grab one of the tangible gifts I'd gotten for her to open as I pulled off.

When I sat it in her lap, she didn't move right away, instead looking at me to ask, "Maverick, what is this?"

"Just open it, Camryn," I insisted, keeping my eyes on the road as I listened to the ruffling of her digging through the gift bag. "I know sneakers aren't necessarily your thing, *but...*"

"You got me Beyoncé *Adidas*?!" she squealed, popping the top off the box to take a closer look as I chuckled, "*Ivy Park*, but yeah. I figured they might be the one pair you'd actually care to have in your closet."

"These are the only shoes I've ever stood in a virtual waiting line for, and I *still* didn't get a pair," she explained, peeking my way with glossy eyes to ask, "How'd you know?"

The fact that the gift selection was on point enough to cause happy tears made me even prouder to share, "Well, I noticed you had a few pieces from the collection still with tags on 'em, so I thought these might give you a reason to finally put 'em in rotation."

"Considering athleisure will probably be the only thing I can fit into this Fall, these are right on time," she added, smiling at the shoes before giving me the same excited grin when she turned to say, "Thank you, baby."

Grabbing her free hand, I kissed her knuckles and told her, "Anything for you. Told you that from day one."

"I don't think either one of us knew *that* would mean *this*," she insisted with a giggle even though I didn't totally agree.

"Speak for yourself, Cam. I been knew what was up. I wasn't just sayin' shit to get the drawers."

I mean, was I thinking about a baby that would propel us into a relationship when I said that to Camryn before we fucked in her office?

Of course not.

But I also didn't think that moment would be the beginning and end of us even though she'd tried her hardest to make it that way after I fumbled our second hook-up, using that as the reason why we couldn't pursue something real until the baby pulled us back together.

It was almost like she'd read my mind once she propped herself up against the center console so that she could challenge, "Even if that is true, do you really think we'd be together right now if it wasn't for the baby?"

"Nah, cause you would've kept playin' me off," I told her honestly, catching the little frown she gave in response like I didn't have evidence.

"Playin' you off? Maverick, you were in a whole relationship up until that week!" she laughed. "And not only that, I legitimately did not think I liked your ass."

"So what changed?"

"You gave up the drawers," she answered, catching a side-eye that made her giggle more as she defended, "I'm joking, I'm joking. I guess I've *just*... gotten to see a different side of you. Or maybe the real you beyond the character I've always had in my head."

Frowning, I asked, "Damn, so you thought of me as a character?"

"More like a profile," she corrected like that made it any

better. "You checked off these certain boxes that automatically made you one thing in my head when you're so much more than that. And the more I learn about you, the more I like."

"You ended that real sweetly, so I'ma let you hoop," I told her. "But for the record, I'm more than a profile."

"Okay, LeBron," she teased as I pulled into a parking spot at her complex, the joke making me chuckle too even as I climbed out of the car and pressed, "I'm serious, Camryn. I experience that way too often. People thinking they know me solely based on what they see on social media. I don't want that with you. I need you to see me for who I really am."

"I do, Maverick," she insisted as I followed her inside. "I know you're not all designer gear and perfectly-lit selfies. You're human. A wonderful, caring, thoughtful human being that I have the pleasure of watching evolve into his next phase."

Hearing her put actual words behind it meant more than she knew, a smile already on my face as she wrapped her arms around my neck to ask, "Now can we get to my next birthday gift in real life, or do I have to settle for a leaked dick pic like the rest of the internet?"

Grabbing her ass, I pulled her as close as her bump allowed when I asked, "You really think you're funny, huh?" Following it up with a peck of a kiss that had Camryn wearing a smirk as she answered, "Just a little bit."

Then she gave me a second kiss that held way more fire, letting me know just how serious she was about that birthday gift as she started guiding us to her bedroom, our lips only disconnecting long enough for me to tell her, "I'm about to tear your funny ass up." And I did, *thoroughly*, forced to pace myself thanks to Camryn's insanely high sex drive that she continuously blamed on the baby.

Either way, I was enjoying every bit of it, enjoying every bit of *her* as we spent the next couple of days together. The first at the spa with Camryn getting a package of treatments that had her more relaxed than I'd ever seen her, and the second at my place, eating pineapple pizza and watching a bunch of movies that Camryn would have to see twice because she couldn't stay awake for any of them.

It was all good, though.

Having her here with me, enjoying herself, was what mattered most. And honestly, with all the time we'd spent together, I found myself missing her on Saturday morning when I sent her to get her hair and nails done for the big surprise; a plan that I'd had to consult Andria on to be able to see through.

Thankfully, now that Andria knew how much I cared about her friend and that I wasn't on any bullshit, she was happy to help me create a guest list of Camryn's closest family and friends who would first meet us for dinner. Then we'd follow that up with a surprise karaoke night back at my place that I'd invited a few of my homies to; the closest thing we could get to a party without having to drag Camryn to a club against her will.

Not that she would've allowed that anyway.

To be real, I was surprised she was going with the flow as much as she had been. But I suppose I'd done a good enough job that she didn't need to be concerned with what was next, giving myself a little pat on the back for getting shit right as I headed to pick her up from her apartment.

I already knew it was going to be a good night when I didn't have my usual hallway run-in with Miss. Lady. But I still wasn't prepared for just how amazing Camryn looked when she opened the door, her curls styled in this fly ass ponytail and the fitted white dress she had on giving off big MILF vibes with a deep V-neck that highlighted both her boobs and her bump.

Simply put, if we didn't have people waiting on us, we wouldn't have been leaving her place. But because we did, I could only show my appreciation with a smile, my stomach feeling fluttery as hell as I asked, "Why does it feel like I have a big ass crush on you right now?"

"Cause you probably do," she insisted with a smile, turning to the mirror to put on a final layer of lip gloss as I slid behind her and agreed, "I definitely do." And from there, I continued watching, wrapping my arms around her waist when I told her, "You look gorgeous, mamas."

"Thank you, Maverick. Now where are we going? I already know my parents are here."

"Ain't no surprising you, huh?" I asked with a laugh, grabbing her hand to insist, "Just come on."

She gave a skeptical look but still did as I asked since she knew I wasn't going to steer her wrong. And by the time we actually got to the restaurant, her parents were the only people she expected to see, caught completely off-guard when she saw that a few of her other family members, some of her friends, and even my own mother and sister were all present.

"Surprise!" they shouted in unison, Camryn hiding her face against my chest in response as I tried to guide her further into the room. And as they all cheered her arrival, I encouraged her to take it all in, her eyes teary as she thanked me before she started giving hugs to everyone in attendance.

While most of them at least knew about the baby by this point, very few had actually seen Camryn's bump in person, making the greetings even longer than usual. But I didn't mind sharing, instead making my way around the room to say what's up to the people I did know; Camryn's parents, Andria, and of course, my own family.

"Y'all are way too cute," was the first thing Malinda said as she pulled me into a hug, my mother giving her own version of the same sentiment before mentioning, "I really hate that you waited until the very last minute to tell me about this, Mav. Got me out here lookin' all regular while everybody else gets to be fine."

"Mama, you look good," I assured her. "And besides, it was kinda a last-minute plan. I'm just glad you could come."

"Wouldn't miss seeing my son this in love for anything," she replied, a curious look on my face as I gave her words some thought just as Camryn approached us with her arms extended to give my mother a hug.

"Ms. Meredith, thank you for comingggg."

"Of course, sweetheart," my mother replied, stepping back to get a better view of Camryn's stomach as she said, "Hate to say I told you so, but look at you now."

"Wait, what?" I thought as Camryn giggled, "I really wanted you to be wrong too, but you sure called it."

"Called what?" I asked, interrupting their little coded back and forth.

Tucking herself under my arm, Camryn explained, "I was sick at the office when your mother came in for a meeting one day. She said I was pregnant, and I didn't want to believe her. But low and behold, the pregnancy tests I picked up that day confirmed her suspicions."

"Tests, plural? Oh, honey. I could've saved you some money," my mother giggled as my curious look remained.

"So my mom knew you were pregnant before I did?"

"Your mom knew I was pregnant before *I* did," Camryn

clarified. "She didn't know that also meant she'd be a grandma, though."

"Actually, I've settled on GiGi. Sounds less... grandma-ish."

With another giggle, Camryn replied, "I'm sure my mama will be coming up with something equally modern."

"Speaking of her, we need to meet. I'd love to have you all over for our monthly brunch tomorrow," my mother mentioned, the fact that she was inviting Camryn to what was usually reserved for family speaking volumes beyond what Camryn even knew as she grabbed both my mom and sister and said, "Come on. I'll introduce you both."

In no time at all, they were off mixing and mingling while I followed to talk sports with Mr. Teddy until dinner was served, the meal lending itself to even more conversation. And as things began to wind down, I interrupted to make a few remarks.

"Before we finish eating, I'd like to thank everybody for coming. I know the invites were a bit last minute, but y'all still showed up for my girl. And as y'all can see from that big ass *Kool-Aid* smile on her face, she really appreciates it."

That caused a murmur of chuckles and a side-eye from Camryn as I spoke directly to her.

"Camryn, while I have everyone's attention, I just wanted to tell you thank you. I know I say it randomly, most times without explanation. But thank you for accepting me. Thank you for challenging me. Thank you for giving my life new purpose, new meaning. Thank you for... allowing me to grow and growing our baby; something I'll never be able to thank you enough for. Thank you for always inspiring me, and inspiring others through your work. Our baby girl, *that we'll find out is a baby girl next week*, is so lucky to have you as her mother. And I'm pretty damn lucky to have you too. Happy Birthday, mamas."

While everybody started giving a succession of, "Awww's" Camryn stood up to pull me into a hug, her eyes glossy when she planted a quick kiss to my lips before whispering, "*Thank you, baby,*" against them. Then I took a seat so that she could give a few remarks of her own.

"Like, Maverick said, thank you all for coming. I've never been this surprised... *well...* I take that back," she giggled with a rub of her belly that made everyone else chuckle too as she continued, "But this was still a nice surprise, so thank you Maverick for pulling this all together. You truly made this the best birthday week ever, and I'll forever be grateful for that."

"We're just gettin' started, mamas," I told her, something everyone else in the room understood as Camryn just responded with a smirk that questioned what I was up to. But she found out soon enough when we pulled up to my place, Camryn already reaching for my zipper as we walked through the door until she saw my apartment filled with everyone from dinner plus a few extra people.

"*Oh my God,*" she groaned embarrassedly, once again burying her face against my chest as Andria teased, "Damn, girl. Now I see how y'all got the first one."

Everybody laughed at that as Camryn playfully smacked me in the chest before asking, "Why didn't you tell me there were going to be people here?"

"I told you we were just gettin' started," I reminded her. "Welcome to the after party."

Because of who was all in attendance, she couldn't help but grin as we made our rounds so that I could introduce her to a few of my homies that I'd invited. But one in particular was missing - *and so was my sister* - a frown on my face as

I left Camryn with her friends on a quest to find Whoa and Malinda who just so happened to walk in from the balcony together.

"Fuck is going on with those two?" I thought from a distance, not getting a chance to completely blow up their spot since Andria was already using the microphone attached to the karaoke machine to kick things off.

"Alright, y'all. As it said in the invite, this isn't some ordinary after party. We're about to turn this bitch... *oop.* Sorry, parents. Turn this *thing* into a full-blown talent show, with every song choice coming from the decade Camryn was born in. So without further ado, I introduce Mr. and Mrs. Cox who are going to perform, "Twisted" by Keith Sweat with Kut Klose."

"Oh, Lord," Camryn sighed from somewhere in the room as her father got on the mic to say, "Cammy Girl, you were almost two when this song first dropped. And you almost got a sibling because of it."

"This song isn't even all that romantic!" she shouted back, everyone in the room cracking up laughing as her parents started their duet. And honestly, they didn't sound half bad.

Not that it took much to sound as good as Keith Sweat.

But as a unit, they sounded pretty good; especially with the rest of the room providing backup since we'd all been raised on the same music.

Making my way back over to Camryn, I wrapped her in a hug from behind and found a little groove, the both of us singing along with her parents until Andria called up the next performer.

"Alright. Now we have Malinda and Ms. Meredith who will be performing, "Downtown" by SWV."

"Aww hell nah," I groaned, the room once again finding

a good laugh as my mother and sister got on the mic and enthusiastically sang a song about eating pussy in front of an audience.

"It's okay. We can be embarrassed together," Camryn insisted with a laugh, dancing in front of me as she sang right along with them. But coming from her, it hit different since, *shit*... I'd be downtown right now if it wasn't for all these people in my spot.

Camryn was enjoying the company, though. So I wasn't about to complain, accepting the performance for what it was before I was called to the mic to perform, "Forever My Lady" by Jodeci with Walter.

Because of house seniority, I sang lead and Whoa backed me up, the two of us being dramatic as hell to everyone's amusement. And Camryn was especially giggly, even more so once I pulled her into the performance so that I could sing to her directly since the lyrics were hella fitting for our situation.

We had a baby on the way, were falling in love, and if it was up to me, she really would be my lady forever. But unfortunately, by the time we woke up to go to brunch the next day, another wrench had already been thrown at my plan.

CAMRYN

I couldn't even eat.

Everybody was telling me not to worry, not to sweat it, insisting that it would all blow over soon. But in the thick of it, none of their advice changed the fact that I was now at the head of Maverick's alleged love square.

The fact that the internet was even calling it that made me sick since that was far from the truth. But according to the multiple videos that one of Maverick's friends had drunkenly posted to his *Instagram* story of the two of us dancing together and then him singing to me, I was just one in the number instead of his actual girlfriend who was carrying his child.

Of course, me being pregnant only made people even more interested in my existence. They were piecing together timelines, estimating when the baby was conceived based on mine and Maverick social media posts and then using that to figure out when I'd be due. They were combing through *Google* to see what came up in the search results about me and my life, someone even going as far as connecting me to the foundation which led to pictures of Maverick and I at the gala being shared. And then there were the Banksy boos finding old ass pictures of Nate and I to say it must've been his baby and that Maverick was just joking around with me as an employee of his family's foundation.

Yeah, shit was a joke alright.

People were coming up with new theories left and right, arguing amongst themselves as Maverick acted like it was all no big deal. And while I could only imagine how jaded he'd become to this sort of nonsense, it just wasn't rolling off my back as easily.

I wanted to defend myself.

I wanted him to defend us.

I wanted all of this shit to go away so that I could just go back to my quiet, private life.

But the reality was, Maverick had warned me.

You can't hide forever, Camryn.

I'd tried, *and failed*, and now I was paying the price of having to deactivate all of my social media accounts and stay off the internet for as long as possible since going up against the masses was a lost cause. But I would've been lying if I didn't admit how tempted I was every other second, ready to say fuck it and just face it head-on instead of ignoring it altogether.

Those were the two options Maverick gave me.

In fact, his exact words were, "We either step right into the spotlight and all that comes with it, or we stay lowkey and let the bulb burn out." And since being in the spotlight wasn't at all what I wanted, I chose the latter, going through the motions of brunch with his family and mine and then forcing myself into a nap that only resulted in me not being able to get real sleep later that night.

That's how I ended up back on social media.

Using the foundation's page like a burner account, I

skipped through a few of the more popular blog sites to see what people were saying about the videos of us that had been shared, surprised to find a mixed bag of responses in the comments section.

Some were super positive.

"He looks so happy!"

"Okay, but they're super cute together."

"Yes, baby bump. #MILFSeason"

Others were flat out mean.

"That dress is super trashy for a pregnant woman."

"She's nowhere near as fine as Lillian or Sophia."

"THAT'S who Maverick got pregnant? Damn, I might've had a chance with him."

And then there were a few that landed somewhere in between.

"I swear this nigga looks madly in love with every girl he's ever been pictured with."

"At least Maverick always keeps a pretty black woman on his arm."

"Can't be mad. Sis secured the bag."

Obviously, I wasn't after Maverick for his money. And anyone who knew me in real life knew that. But it still bothered me that *that* could be treated as a valid theory worth investigating while no one even came close to speculating the truth.

Not that the truth was perfect, or even ideal. But there was still plenty of beauty to it; especially when you took into account all of the events of the past week.

The thoughtfulness, the gifts, the choice of activities that were right up my alley.

The balance of time spent with each other, and then with family and friends.

The love.

Maverick didn't have to say those exact words for me to feel it through his actions. And I didn't have to say it back since the shit was practically oozing out of my pores. But now, thanks to his little friend, instead of basking in the glow of the weekend, I was dreading having to get out of bed and go to work in a few hours.

The little bit of sleep I got only made for a groggy morning that had Janet concerned enough to ask, "Camryn, are you feeling okay? Should we give your doctor a call?"

Shaking my head, I yawned and answered, "Nothing's wrong with the baby, Janet. I just didn't get much sleep last night."

"Still wired from all that partying, huh?" she questioned teasingly. "Brett and I surely would've been there if we hadn't left town for a quick getaway."

"Yeah, we had fun. But *it's...* not that," I told her, releasing a sigh that I followed with, "Can I ask you something?"

Chuckling, she replied, "That's a question in itself, but sure. What's on your mind?"

"So you've had a famous sister for a very long time. How did you manage to stay out of the spotlight? I mean, you've still lived a relatively private life, right?"

"Relatively, yes," she answered with a nod. "Do most people around here know I'm Meredith Woods's sister? They do. But do people bother me about it? Not really."

Hearing her response pinpointed the real issue. The only reason I'd had to keep things under wraps with Maverick was because people couldn't just know and be quiet. They had to bother, and dissect, and entertain themselves with other people's lives instead of worrying about their own. And it was almost like she could read my mind the way she continued, "You kids have it so differently now. With all the phones, and social media, it's much harder to fly under the radar. But back when Meredith was first coming up, we got to party, and get in trouble, and make our mistakes mostly in peace."

"Sounds like a dream," I sighed, making Janet chuckle again as she went on to say, "Now don't get me wrong. Social media isn't all bad. You all are connected in a way that we never could be, and you can do a lot of good with that. But having the whole world know you just popped a piece of gum in your mouth long before the flavor even runs out? That's a scary thing."

"Yeah, Maverick and I were sharing a very private moment, in the comfort of his home. And it was already circulating online by the next morning," I told her, permanently annoyed with Maverick's "friend" as Janet gasped, "*Oh Lord*. A sex tape?"

"*What*? No!" I squealed, feeling silly when I explained, "We were just dancing and stuff."

With a wave of her hand, she concluded, "Oh, that's not so bad. I mean, what could possibly be the problem with dancing?"

"Well... people didn't know about Maverick and me as a couple. And they surely didn't know about the baby. So now it's turned into a whole thing of who I am, who he's actually dating, if it's his baby, etc., etc."

Being the talk of the internet was honestly surreal, especially since I'd done everything I could to avoid it up until this point. But according to Janet, the solution to my problem lied within the problem itself, a grin on her face when she asked, "Want to know the other good part about social media? You can take control of your own narrative, *instantly*. You don't have to wait for a magazine to run a story, or for some fancy PR statement to be distributed to the appropriate media channels. You can shut all the noise down with a single post. Drop the mic on their asses."

I responded with a laugh because Janet wasn't a huge swearer meaning she was dead serious about what she was saying. Still, I had some concerns, namely, "You don't think that's just inviting more people into my business, though? You know, stoking the fire by giving them even more to talk about?"

"Would you rather them continue to tell it, or you?"

Her question was valid. But I also couldn't shake the fact that I shouldn't have been obligated to explain myself to a bunch of strangers since it wasn't supposed to matter what they thought.

It did matter, though.

Not necessarily what they thought. But that the truth was out there somewhere even if they chose to bury it with more lies. And with Janet's advice and pep talk brewing in my head for the rest of the day, I found myself fired up enough to make a whole post by the time I got home from work, bypassing the flurry of notifications that came with reactivating my *Instagram* account so that I could share my favorite picture from my birthday dinner of Maverick and me kissing after his adorable speech.

"Best Birthday Ever. Thank you, @MaverickWoods. <3"

If this were ordinary times with an ordinary man, it would've been taken for what it was.

A cute ass picture.

But because of the circumstances, I found myself nervous to actually press the "share" button, knowing it would probably be the start of a new wave of mayhem.

My finger was literally hovering the screen when I heard heavy pounding at my front door, my phone falling from my hand as I whispered, *"What the hell..."* before crawling off the couch to see what was going on. And once I saw who was on the other side, I was instantly furious, yanking the door open to ask, "Nate, what are you doing here?"

"The baby," he answered. "Is it mine?"

My frown only tightened at his question, my eyebrows

furrowed when I crossed my arms and responded, "Are you drunk?"

"Answer me, Camryn!" he yelled, making me jump a bit before I annoyedly told him, "No, Nate. Do the math. If it was your baby, I'd be a lot further along in my pregnancy."

"Is he the reason why we can't get back together?"

Wait, what?

Him showing up to question my pregnancy was one thing; a dumb thing, but still a thing that I could stretch to find some sort of explanation behind. But now he was coming at me about Maverick?

"Is that why you're really here? You see me *finally* receiving the kinda love you refused to give, and it's too much for you to handle?" I asked, taking a step out of my apartment so that I could poke him in the chest and make things clear. "Maverick isn't the reason why we'll never get back together, Nate. You are!"

Grabbing my hand, he stepped as close as he could to beg, "Camryn, please. I don't care about the baby. We can raise it together. I *just*... I want you back so bad."

What the...

"Fuck is goin' on here?" Maverick asked, the sound of his voice enough to startle me into creating some space between Nate and me.

"Maverick! *Hey*. I didn't know you were coming by."

"And I didn't know he was coming by," Maverick replied, his eyes already burning into Nate when he asked, "Is there a problem, man?"

"Actually, there is," Nate answered, running a hand over his bald head before he got right in Maverick's face to say, "You."

Maverick responded by shoving Nate in the chest, Nate coming back at him with a punch that Maverick thankfully dodged before tackling Nate to the ground. And I almost couldn't believe the sight in front of me, the two of them tussling like big ass kids and making enough noise to draw the attention of my nosy neighbor.

"Oh my God! Will y'all stop?!" I begged from a distance since the last thing I wanted to do was accidentally put myself and the baby in danger. But once I saw blood coming from Maverick's face and Nate's eye beginning to swell, I knew I had to intervene; especially after I heard my neighbor cheering, "Ooh! Get 'em, Nate! I mean, Maverick! I mean... *wait a minute.*"

I was on my way to break it up when Maverick stood up over Nate and groaned, "Fuck outta here, nigga," literally dragging him out of the door before coming back my way to ask, "You aight, Cam?"

"Yeah, *I'm...* I'm fine," I answered breathily. "But your face..."

"Bitch ass nigga scratched me," Maverick spat, swiping at the blood dripping from the deep scratch under his eye before deciding, "I should go out there and beat his ass again for that weak ass shit."

"*No.* No more fighting," I told him, grabbing him by the arm so that I could pull him into my apartment. Then I guided him to the bathroom so that we could do something about his scratch, the sight of it making me cringe as I started applying pressure to stop the bleeding while Maverick just stared at me.

"Why was he here, Camryn?"

"I don't know. He just showed up out of the blue," I answered, getting ready to wash the cut with soap and water until Maverick pressed, "You tellin' the truth?"

"Are you really questioning that?" I asked, frowning as I reminded him, "All the suspect shit I've taken your word on, and you still think I'd make up a lie about Nate's dumb ass?"

"I'm not sayin' that. I just think it's a little strange, is all," he explained in this weirdly calm tone that left me bothered, only adding to that feeling when he said, "Just answer me this. Were you about to kiss that nigga? Yes or no."

"Of course not!" I yelled, legitimately offended when I went on to ask, "Why would you even think something like that?"

"Cause that's exactly what it looked like when I walked up, Camryn."

"The same way all of those pictures... *you know what?* No," I told him, quickly deciding, "I'm not about to let you stress me out any more than I already am. So if this is what you came over here for, you can go."

As far as his scratch care was concerned, he could handle that shit himself cause I was done, retreating to the living room to calm myself down with Maverick eventually following to join me on the couch. And after a few moments of silence between us, he finally spoke, "I didn't come here to stress you out, Camryn. I was actually coming to do the exact opposite."

"By beating up my ex and then accusing me of doing slick shit with him behind your back?"

"Neither of those were in my plans," he sighed, grabbing my hands to add, "And while I'm not sorry for walkin' ol' boy like the dog he is, I am sorry for making it seem like I don't trust you. I *do* trust you, Camryn."

Hearing him proclaim it now didn't exactly erase how irritated I was with him for insinuating that nonsense in the first place. But I did appreciate the sentiment enough to respond, "You need a *Band-Aid.* And some *Neosporin.*"

"Can you help me out?" he asked with a bit of a grin

that made me roll my eyes as I stood up from the couch and groaned, "I guess."

"*Camryn...*"

"What, Maverick?" I tossed over my shoulder as he followed me back to the bathroom. "You're lucky Lucille doesn't know how to hold her phone steady, or our asses would've probably ended up on the blogs... *again.*"

Honestly, even though it hadn't happened, just the thought of something like this popping up on the internet still gave me a headache. Though Maverick was stuck on the mention of my neighbor when he asked, "That's her name?"

Instead of answering his question, I focused on gathering the supplies we needed, the sight of his scratch as I dabbed it with ointment making me shake my head as I playfully mentioned, "I can't believe y'all were really fighting over me like that."

Sure, it might've been a battle of egos more than anything. But it still felt good to hear Maverick say, "I wear this scratch proudly, mamas. I'll do anything to defend what's mine."

While I could argue that he hadn't exactly done enough defending with the folks online, I realized in that moment that him stepping up in real life meant so much more than that. Him going to actual blows with someone who called themselves trying to threaten our relationship, *protecting me*, was much bigger than him continuing to use pictures and captions to argue with strangers on *Instagram*. And though that should've given me every reason to follow his lead in that regard, it felt more important for me to defend what was mine by grabbing my phone and finally pressing "share".

MAVERICK

To say I missed Camryn was an understatement.

Now that we'd made it through the storm of being unexpectedly outed, *and I'd stopped kickin' it with the nigga who'd done that stupid shit in the first place*, we were in a much better place both privately and publicly. And that only made it harder for me to spend my Thursday through Sunday traveling to host parties week after week instead of spending that time with her, my body here with the people who were paying me but my heart back home with Camryn and our baby girl.

Yeah, that shit was finally official and I couldn't have been happier, already missing talking to her in utero and the random little kicks she was starting to give. And Camryn wasn't making shit any easier on me, posting sweet pictures on *Instagram* of her posed in the mirror with her belly popping through her half-buttoned pajama shirt and the caption, **"Keily's Mama <3"**

I couldn't get in her comments fast enough, gassing the hell out of her when I let my fingers fly across the screen like I wasn't in the middle of the club.

"Keily's Mama bad as hell."

"Why you so fine, tho?"

"#AllMine #NewScreensaverAlert"

Of course, now that we'd forced people to accept the fact that Camryn and I were together, *happily*, they were all for the love I was showing her, my notifications full of people "liking" and replying to my comment with their own about how cute we were. And while it felt good not having to go up against them for a change, it felt even better to get a special picture from Camryn of her wearing a little less than the pajama shirt followed by the text, **"Miss you, papa ;)"**

"Gotdamn, girl. Why you playin' with me like this?" - Maverick

"I just miss you is all :(." - Camryn

"I miss you more, mamas. Coming your way the second I get back tomorrow." - Maverick

Grinning at the single heart emoji she'd responded with, I was getting ready to scroll back up to the picture she'd sent me until I heard someone ask, "Am I trippin', or does this feel like a set-up?"

Turning to see if the face matched the voice, I was somehow still surprised to see, "Lillian?"

"Damn. Do I look that different?" she asked with a giggle, running her fingers through the new lavender bob she was rocking as opposed to the usual long, straight, and black weave the world knew her for. And it wasn't only that that had changed, her entire swag a bit more edgy and relaxed compared to the picture-perfect shit she used to be after.

She just looked... comfortable, *in a good way*, making it easy for me to smile when I finally answered, "I mean, yeah. *Sort of.* The hair, obviously. But I guess I'm just more surprised to see you *here* of all places."

"A girl goes to rehab and suddenly can't have fun anymore?" she questioned with another laugh before adding, "Substance-free fun, of course. And now that I have the right kind of support in my circle, that's much easier to stick to. Not that you're some awful person for the times we had, *but...*"

Holding my hand up, I interjected, "I get it. No need to explain."

With a nod, Lillian went on to say, "Crazy as it sounds, even though this was not at all planned, you being here at my first public appearance actually feels a bit full circle. I mean, if it wasn't for you breaking up with me, I might've never gotten the help I needed. Never found this place of really being able to enjoy myself without being out of my damn mind. So thank you, Mav. Seriously."

While she'd managed to frame it in a nice way, being

thanked for breaking up with somebody was still some weird shit that had my face a bit scrunched when I replied, "Glad I could help, Lillian."

"And I'm glad I could get out of the way of you finding true love," she added. "Cause you and Camryn are like... *disgustingly* adorable."

Naturally, that brought my smile back. "We are a pretty good look, huh?"

"The best kind of look. Like, if I didn't already have my own thing going on, I might actually be a little jealous. Matter of fact..."

Giving a wave to get someone's attention, she invited a woman over to where we were standing, waiting for her to join us before she introduced, "Maverick, meet my girl-friend, Zena."

"Girlfriend? *Nice*," I said, once again trying to play off yet another surprise as I extended my hand to say, "Good to meet you, Zena."

"And you as well, Maverick. I've heard so much about you. Maybe too much."

"Just don't tell anybody," I replied with a chuckle. "They're already about to be on my ass for talkin' to your girl here."

With another wave of her hand, Lillian insisted, "Don't worry. I'll take care of it."

What exactly she meant by that, I wasn't sure. But I knew I'd need it when I finally got back to town and was greeted by an irritated Camryn who didn't even bother saying hi when she let me into her apartment.

"*Damn.* Hello to you too."

Instead of responding with any sort of warm welcome, she replied, "Could've at least warned me, Maverick."

"Warned you about what?"

"That you and Lillian were going to be in the club together," Camryn answered, making me release a heavy sigh since... *damn, I guess I could've warned her.*

While I'd rightfully assumed that the lurkers would pull *something* from the brief conversation I'd had with Lillian, I knew I hadn't done anything even remotely suspect worth speculating about.

No hugs.

No touching.

I was extra careful in making sure there were no romantic vibes whatsoever. And not only that, but it was a surprise to both Lillian and I that we'd ended up in the same place, a fact that seemed important enough to share.

"I didn't even know she was going to be there until she rolled up on me in VIP. And she introduced me to her girl-friend shortly after."

"Lillian has a girlfriend?" Camryn asked, watching me nod as I told her, "It was news to me too. She seemed happy, though."

"Trust me. I could tell how happy she was from the pictures," she replied with a roll of her eyes before finding the post on her phone to show me. And while the actual photo of Lillian and I wasn't at all damning, the caption suggested something totally different.

"**#ComebackQueen We have exclusive pictures of Lillian Banks on her first night out since completing her rehabilitation program, and sis looks BOMB. New haircut and color, new wardrobe, and a new ass that was enough to grab the attention of her supposedly taken ex who was also in the building. Is there trouble in pregnant paradise? We'll let you scroll and be the judge.**"

Shaking my head, I went down to the comments and saw what must've been a new one from Lillian herself.

"@LillianBanks : First of all, my ass is fat from eating good, working out, and not doing drugs lol. And second of all, if y'all weren't trying so hard to make something out of nothing, you'd see I was clearly introducing Maverick to a woman. My woman :)"

In that moment, I realized what Lillian had meant about "taking care of it" since she'd very intentionally taken the attention off of Camryn and I and put it on herself and her new relationship. And while I could only imagine how the move would kick-off the perfect reintroduction for her, right now it was going to be used for the sole purpose of helping me out of this jam as I showed it to Camryn while telling her, "Crazy enough, we were joking about this exact shit when this picture was taken."

"Glad to see you two still have things to joke about," she replied with another roll of her eyes that had me quick to ask, "Camryn, you're not really trippin' about this little shit, are you?"

"No. *Of course not.* I love seeing pictures of my boyfriend and his ex in a club together hundreds of miles away while I'm sitting at home, *alone*, using my third-trimester belly as a napkin to hold my *Cheetos*."

So that's what this was really about.

She believed that I wasn't on any funny shit with Lillian - *a good thing*. But now that we were almost thirty weeks deep, she was growing more weary and irritable, a playful frown on my face as I pulled her into a hug with a groaned, "Aww, poor baby."

"I'm tired of being pregnant," she whined into my chest. "I wanna have fun too."

"We'll have plenty of fun at the baby shower next weekend," I insisted. Though she was quick to counter, "Non-pregnant fun, Maverick. With alcohol, and sexy clothes, and dick from positions other than behind."

Frowning, I asked, "You don't like when I hit that shit from the back?"

"I love when you hit it from the back," she sighed. "But I'm pretty sure I'm gonna hate it by the time the baby is due."

"Nah, I'll never let you hate it," I told her confidently, ready for my "welcome home" fill as I started kissing on her neck. And even though she wasn't at all resisting it, she still whined, "Maverick, stop. I'm not in the mood."

"Quit lyin'. You're always in the mood," I suggested, getting all the proof I needed when she pulled my face down to hers for a kiss while I safely guided us over to the couch. And after easing her way down, she was strategic about getting rid of her pajama shorts and panties even while claiming, "I should be mad at you right now."

"You're not, though."

"I am a little bit."

Pulling my shirt off, I dropped to my knees and replied, "Nah, not even."

"Yes, I... *shiiiiit*."

The rest of her words turned to gibberish as I ate her pussy like I missed it - *because I did* - flicking my tongue against her swollen pearl as she grabbed the back of my head to hold me exactly where she wanted me. And even though she was being mad aggressive with it, I loved that shit, matching the energy while also staying mindful of how far she was stretching her back so that she wouldn't hurt herself.

Not that she cared.

For Camryn, this was about one thing and one thing only by any means necessary. And I was more than happy to get her there, *safely*, her legs draped over my shoulders as I ate her pussy until she cried my name and my beard was left covered in her juices.

"Still don't want me to hit that shit from the back?" I asked teasingly once I finally pulled away to get the rest of my clothes off, Camryn's tone dangerously low when she replied, "If you don't get that dick inside of me right now, I'm gonna rip it off of you and use it like a dildo."

"Gotdamn, Camryn. Now it's scared of you," I laughed, though it wasn't exactly a lie since my dick was acting a little shy once I got out of my boxers. But Camryn was more than willing to make up for her threats, sitting up towards the edge of the couch to tell me - *or it* -, "I'm sorry. Come here."

Once I got close enough, she palmed my dick and started stroking it in her hand, leaning forward even more so that she could tease the tip with her tongue. And after I took a single step closer towards the couch, she was able to swallow me whole, the feel of her mouth making it hard for me to remain standing as I gripped into her shoulder and let out a long, "*Fuuuuck.*"

Like she was on a mission, she stayed aggressive when giving me head, my hand buried in her hair as encourage-ment for her to go off. And she did, getting so into it that my toes were clinching onto the carpet by the time I warned,

"Come get this dick before you fuck around and turn my baby into a cannibal."

With a mischievous smirk, she wiped her mouth and pushed herself up from the couch so that she could turn around. And once she was positioned comfortably, I slipped inside of her wet ass pussy with a shared moan.

Now I was really home.

In an attempt to be careful, I started off by taking it slow. But Camryn wasn't having that, throwing her ass back on me and begging me to fuck her harder. So I did, unable to hold back in giving her everything she wanted, even when I teased, "You hate it from the back yet?"

"No. I love it. I love *you*."

"You love me?"

"I love you, baby," she repeated breathily, gripping into the couch as I continued to crash her shit from behind and replied, "I love you too, Camryn. *Forever*."

That was real shit, not sex talk. But I would've been lying if I didn't admit how hearing those few words fueled me into taking things up an extra notch that had Camryn loud as hell when she finally came. And once I did the same, I was confident that we'd both need a nap; though Camryn was acting like she wasn't done once she made her way off the couch and started kissing me again.

If I had to expedite my reboot for her pleasure, I would. But the more she kissed me, the more my face started itching, distracting me enough to ask, "Why the fuck are my lips feelin' so tingly?"

"*Oooh.* I forgot about that," she sighed, already looking guilty as hell when I pressed, "You forgot about what?"

Avoiding my eyes, she released another sigh before she answered, "I ate some peanut *M&Ms* earlier. Cause I was mad at you."

"So you tried to kill me?" I asked, rubbing my nose and lips to alleviate the itching as she defended, "You said your peanut allergy was mild!"

"That's not the point," I groaned as she took off towards the bathroom and I followed, grateful to see she already had some *Benadryl* on deck along with an apology.

"I'm sorry. These pregnancy mood swings are a bitch."

Shaking my head, I quickly swallowed down two pills before telling her, "Nah, don't blame the baby. Your ass been crazy. I still ain't forgot about the scissors incident."

"And now I'll never be able to forget what else happened in that office," she replied with a sweet smile, rubbing her naked belly like that was supposed to make me forget what she'd just done.

It didn't.

My face was still itching too much for that.

But the fact that I was patiently waiting for the *Benadryl* to kick in instead of being pissed the fuck off made one thing certain.

I was madly in love with Camryn CrazyAss Cox.

CAMRYN

Keily's father was doing the absolute most.
The Burberry shirt.
The camera crew.
The DJ.
The swag bags.

All money that could've been spent on stuff for the baby, but instead had been spent turning my baby shower into some soft pink and gold coed extravaganza that would've annoyed me if the shit wasn't so cute and I wasn't confident he could afford it.

Truthfully, it wasn't even all his money, his mother, my parents, and Andria all teaming up to bring what was ultimately Maverick's vision to life. And considering I didn't have to lift a single finger, I wasn't about to complain, smiling for all the footage, being especially gracious when opening gifts, and completely devouring all the finger foods that were more than likely going to give me heartburn.

It was worth it, though.

Baby girl thought so too, clearly her father's child since

she was also doing the most up against my bladder. And only because I loved them both was I taking it in the stride, breaking away from the crowd for a quick trip to the bathroom and barely making it back out of the door without Maverick hounding me to ask, "Hey, you okay?"

His concern was enough to make giggle. "I'm fine, Mav. Just had to pee."

"Okay, good," he sighed like he was relieved before brushing his hand against my chubbier than usual cheek to compliment, "You look so damn beautiful, Camryn."

"And you *look*… like a baby daddy at a baby shower."

"Not just any baby daddy," he suggested, giving a smirk when he pulled me into his arms and corrected, "Your proud ass baby daddy."

"More like, my *fine* ass baby daddy," I replied, sneaking a kiss that had my father intervening from a distance when he yelled, "Hey, y'all two cut it out now!"

Giggling against Maverick's lips, we made our way back to the shower that was thankfully wrapping up since I was truly exhausted. And by the time we said our thank you's and got Maverick's truck loaded up with all the gifts, I was barely able to keep my eyes open, my phone the only thing keeping me awake since it wouldn't stop buzzing.

"All these notifications," I groaned, easily concluding, "You must've posted something."

Originally, we'd decided we would wait until we got the pictures back from the professional photographer Maverick had hired before we shared anything from the baby shower online. But apparently, Maverick had already thrown that plan in the trash while also managing to throw my friend under the bus when he weakly defended, "Blame Andria. She's the one who took that fire ass pic knowing I wouldn't be able to help myself."

Rolling my eyes, I opened the *Instagram* app so that I could see the picture he was talking about, immediately recognizing why he'd been so pressed to share it since it was literal perfection. A candid moment of the two of us laughing together while he held my belly from behind.

"Oh, this is super cute," I agreed before glancing at the caption. "*Awww*. You and your favorite girls. You're gonna make GiGi Meredith and TT Mali jealous."

That made Maverick smirk as I continued down to the comments and was surprised to see that Lillian had already left one that was drawing thousands of likes.

"@LillianBanks : Literally dying from all this cuteness! @CammyCC is so gorg!"

Of course, people were responding with applause for her maturity while I thought it was a bit overdone. But instead of making a big deal about it, I "liked" both the picture and the comment before moving on to "like" all the pictures my real-life friends had shared from the shower, a big smile on my face as I scrolled through the freshly-made memories until we pulled up to Maverick's place.

"I'll come grab all this stuff later," he announced. "But first, I wanna show you somethin'."

I had no idea what he was talking about as he first led us into the complex, then into his apartment, and finally into his former shoe room where I gasped, "Maverick, oh my God..."

Grinning bashfully, he asked, "What you think? You like it?"

"It's beautiful," I sighed as I took in the nursery he'd put together, the soft pink and gold scheme used throughout the room identical to the one he'd used for the baby shower with touches of white that popped amongst the color.

The space was comfortable and functional, with all the furniture needed for a newborn, a library of baby books, and the letters of our baby's name hanging on the wall above the crib. And of course, *because it was Maverick*, there was already a collection of shoes, knitted versions of popular sneakers that were so tiny and cute I almost started crying just imagining them on Keily's feet.

Honestly, the more I looked around, the more I realized, "I don't know how I'm even gonna be able to compete with all this back at my place."

"Or *maybe...* you don't have to compete," Maverick suggested, wrapping me in a hug from behind when he casually added, "Maybe you can just move here. With me. I mean, it would only make sense, right?"

Immediately, I frowned. "Make sense for me to give up my space to join you in yours? I don't know, Maverick."

"Don't think of it like that," he insisted. "Think of it like, giving Keily one house filled with love instead of splitting the love between the two."

Giggling, I turned around to face him when I replied, "I'm not worried about the love our baby will receive, Mav. I'm worried about what us two living under the same roof - *your roof* - will look like."

"Not much different than it looks when I'm spending every other night at your spot and you're spending the opposite days at mine," he answered with a shrug that had me quick to counter, "Actually, it's very different than that. Cause at the end of the day, we still have our own space."

Sure, I kept a few things at Maverick's place and he kept a few things at mine. And yes, we tended to bounce back and forth between the two spots. But that still wasn't the same as full-on moving in together, a decision I couldn't take lightly even with the pressure of Maverick's heated glare once he asked, "So you're sayin' you don't wanna live with me?"

"I'm *saying* this is just a lot to think about, and that I'm not prepared to give you a definite answer right at this moment."

It seemed like a fair response to me, but I could tell Maverick was disappointed when he somberly replied, "*Fine*," already turning to leave the room as he said, "I'm gonna go get the gifts from the car." And he did, taking his sweet time to do so and leaving me alone in my thoughts until he returned wearing the same somber look that made it impossible for me not to say something.

"Maverick, I'm really not trying to hurt your feelings. But you have to understand where I'm coming from on this."

Even if he didn't like it, I knew it wasn't some farfetched thing for me to need a little time to think things through first. But it didn't take long for me to realize it wasn't about my thought process at all, more about Maverick's ego once he responded, "You not really fuckin' with your boy like that. Message received."

"Oh, stop it. You know it's not that," I groaned, Maverick getting right in my face to ask, "Then what is it, Camryn?"

His closeness made my heart race as I tried to find the words to explain myself, hoping it made sense once I finally spoke, "This place is just so yours that I don't really see where I fit. And my place is so mine that there's not really room for you there either."

"I'll clear all this shit out and we can start over from

scratch if that's what it takes," he suggested, making me giggle as I pulled him closer to respond, "I love the enthusiasm, baby. I really do. *Just...* give me some time to think about it, okay?"

"Yeah, aight," he groaned unconvincingly, forcing me to scold, "*Maverick...*"

"I said aight, Camryn. Take all the time you need," he offered before quickly amending, "*Well...* not all the time cause baby girl will be here before we know it, but..."

"Just a day or two. Three days max," I told him, knowing any more than that would probably drive the both of us crazy. And thankfully, he agreed, allowing us to spend the rest of the night without the pressure of making any decisions.

Those three days went by fast as hell, though. And while Maverick hadn't at all pressed me about it, I knew it was coming soon enough, my mind somehow still torn as I spent time with Andria sorting through all the clothes she'd bought for Keily.

Because she knew me well, it was easy for her to pick up on the fact that something was weighing on me heavily. But once I presented everything to her, she made it sound like a no-brainer when she replied, "Girl, if you don't pack your shit up and go before this baby comes."

"Andi, it's really not that simple," I sighed, only for Andria to immediately counter, "Yes it is, Cammy Cammie Cam. You love that man. He loves you. Baby Keily is like, two months from making her grand debut, and a ready-for-action nursery is *where*? At his place."

"Exactly. *His place.* Not ours," I emphasized. Though, once again, Andria was quick to offer a rebuttal.

"O-kay. So put your touches on it and make it y'alls, Camryn."

"It's already been touched," I replied with a subtle eye roll that Andria caught enough of to conclude, "Ahh, so that's your issue. The bachelor pad is a little too bachelor-reminiscent for you."

It wasn't even that I was trying to hold Maverick's past against him. That wouldn't be fair. And it wasn't like we hadn't made our own wonderful memories there too. But I still couldn't shake what that apartment represented for him, a frown on my face as I explained, "I mean, it's one thing for us to chill there. Sleep there on occasion. But to actually live there? As a family? I don't know, Andi."

With Andria nodding along, I continued, "And even if it was the opposite way, there's no way he could move all his shit in here."

Just the thought made me feel claustrophobic as Andria agreed, "Yeah, he'd be better off living in a storage unit."

"Shut up," I giggled while Andria went on to say, "Seriously, though. I know nothing about this has been ideal for you, but everything has still worked out favorably. I can't imagine this being any different."

She'd made an excellent point.

Everything about this situation had gone out of the, *"First comes love, then comes marriage..."* order I'd always had for myself in my head. Every step of the way, there had been different challenges that I thought I for sure wanted no parts of. But somehow, we'd conquered them anyway, we grew anyway, we figured it out anyway, we fell in love *anyway*. And while that might've been the biggest "oops" of all, it was also the reason why I was giving this idea a second thought, easily concluding that, *like with everything else*, it would work itself out.

Maverick would make sure of it.

Releasing a heavy sigh, I told Andria, "You're right. And

I mean, I really *don't* wanna compete with that nursery. It's so perfect."

The set-up of the room was still clear enough in my head for me to already be imagining myself there as Andria groaned, "So mad you didn't take any pics."

"Well you'll be seeing it soon enough when you come visit Keily and I in our new home," I replied, saying it out loud somehow making it more real even though I'd yet to give Maverick my final decision.

Now that I had one, I couldn't wait to tell him. But when I finally made it over to his place a few hours later and was able to walk right in because his door was being held open by moving boxes, I started to worry I'd taken too long, a concerned look on my face as I found Maverick standing amongst chaos in what used to be the baby's room.

"Maverick, what's going on? What happened to the nursery?" I asked, my frown being met with a grin as Maverick stepped over the mess to meet me in the doorway where he grabbed my hands and posed a question of his own.

"Do you trust me?"

"What does that have to..."

"I asked you a question, Camryn," he interjected before I could finish. And while I had no idea where he was going with any of this, I still gave a nod.

"Yes, Maverick. I trust you."

That made his smile grow wider as he kept one of my hands in his and led me out of his apartment, only confusing me even more as we continued down the hall until he stopped us at the front door of a corner unit.

"Welcome home, mamas."

"*What?*"

Fetching a set of keys from his pocket, he used them to enter the space that was similar in style to his current apartment, but bigger.

Much bigger.

There were three bedrooms instead of two. Walk-in closets that could've easily doubled as dens. Even the kitchen looked like it belonged in a house instead of an apartment. But I still didn't know exactly what any of it meant until Maverick said, "I gave some thought to what you said, and you were right. No matter what, it would've always been my place that you moved into or vice versa. *Not ours.* So I talked to my landlord, and he was more than happy to set us up with a more spacious, more expensive unit that we can make our own. *Together.*"

My eyes pooled with tears as I really started to process what was going on. Not only had Maverick taken the time to understand my qualm, but he'd also gone out of his way to ease my worries by doing something completely extreme, borderline irrational, and yet somehow so perfectly him.

I loved him.

And I loved the place, feeling beyond grateful as I happily sobbed, "Maverick, I don't even know what to say,"

"Say yes, Camryn."

Giggling through my tears, I reminded him, "Last time I said yes to you like this, I ended up pregnant."

"Well this time, you'll end up with keys to our new place in your hand," he insisted, wrapping me in a hug from behind to ask, "So…?"

"Yes, Maverick," I answered proudly, turning around to face him when I added, "But only under one condition."

"Name it."

"*That sectional?*" I asked, waiting for the recognition to

register on his face before I told him, "It can't come with us. Cause I just have a feeling that it's seen some things, *and...*"

Instead of letting me finish, he interrupted with a smirk and the only words I needed to hear.

"Anything for you, Camryn."

MAVERICK

The last two months had flown by.

Between getting moved out of our old places and into the new one, staying consistent with birthing classes, celebrating holidays with friends and family, and then taking on the increase in prenatal appointments as we got closer to Camryn's due date, there was so much going on. And yet, even with all the busyness, it was still some of the happiest times of my life.

I had my girl.

We had our spot.

She was being induced first thing in the morning which meant we'd soon have our baby.

Things were really falling into place for me, and I was more grateful than I'd ever been. Though I had to admit, I was also nervous as fuck.

There were a lot of changes that had happened over the course of Camryn's pregnancy, but none of them were as major as the one that was about to occur tomorrow; an official leap into the title I wouldn't take lightly even though I hadn't grown up with one myself.

Not that I was fazed by it anymore.

My mama made sure of that.

But now that I was getting ready to be a father, I was starting to question if I really had what it took to do right by Keily's upbringing, all the studying in the world not exactly the same as growing up with an example to mimic.

My uncle Brett was a cool male figure in my life, but him and Auntie J didn't have any kids, so I never got to see him being an actual parent. I had homies with fathers, but it wasn't like I'd witnessed them doing the dad thing all that recently. And even the friends I had who were already fathers, most of them I had to stop fuckin' with cause they were treating that shit like a *"when I want to"* instead of a *"have to"*.

I'd never do that to Keily. And I damn sure wouldn't do that to Camryn which was why it was so important to me for us to move in together so that we could truly share the responsibility. But even being in position, I still wasn't as confident as I wanted to be, needing some reinforcement as I climbed out of bed and hit up one of the few people I knew might have the advice I was looking for.

"What's good, Mr. Teddy? Sorry for callin' you so late."

Unsurprisingly, his voice was loaded with concern when he asked, "Camryn ain't already in labor, is she?"

"Nah, she's good. She's sleep," I told him before getting to the point of my call. "I was actually wondering if me and you could talk. Man to man. Future father to vet."

While I hadn't known Mr. Teddy long, in the time that I had known him it was evident how great of a father he was. And not only that, but he was a real one on every level, somebody I could count on to give it to me straight after asking, "What's on your mind, youngblood?"

Releasing a sigh, I answered, "I guess I'm just nervous, man. Wondering if I'll be any good at this parenting shit."

"Why wouldn't you be? I mean, you know how to care for somebody, don't you?"

"I do," I replied with a nod he couldn't see. "But I know being a dad is about a lot more than just caring."

"Are there other technicalities? Yeah, nigga. *Obviously.* But at the most basic level, all Keily is gonna want is for you to care, meet her needs, and let her know she's loved no matter what."

The way he'd broken it down made it sound so simple, though I still had my concerns; especially since, "I know raising Camryn couldn't have *possibly* been as easy as that."

That made him chuckle. "I was still a kid myself when we had Camryn. Didn't have a dad, so I didn't know what that shit was even supposed to look like. But on a human level, there's just certain things we all need. So from the second she popped outta her mama's coota cat, I made it my mission to provide that for Camryn in the best way I knew how."

Knowing how well that had worked out for him, I would've been a fool to take his words lightly, a smile on my face as I complimented, "Well you did your thing, oldhead. That girl is a beast."

"Yeah, that's my baby girl," he agreed proudly. "A love like no other from the second I laid eyes on her. You'll see what I mean soon enough."

"What you mean soon enough? I already love Camryn to death," I defended, feeling like a fool once Mr. Teddy groaned, "I'm talking about Keily, nigga."

"Oh. *Right.* My bad," I chuckled, Mr. Teddy laughing too as he advised, "Get some sleep, Mav. I promise you you're gonna need that shit."

"Nah, you right," I told him, making sure to show love when I added, "I appreciate the pep talk, though. For real."

"Ain't no problem, man. We'll see y'all tomorrow."

Ending the call, I felt a little better about everything until I came back in the bedroom and found Camryn sitting up wide awake. And while it was my natural reaction to be concerned, she was the first to ask, "Hey, you okay?"

Joining her back in the bed, I answered, "Yeah, I'm good. What you doin' up? I thought you were asleep."

"I was until your daughter decided to throw herself a going-away party," she sighed, the both of us glancing down at her stomach just in time to see the baby trying to move around.

Shit was creepy and fascinating all at once, Camryn's skin stretching every which way as I teased, "Looks like she's ready for the spotlight."

"Just like her damn daddy," Camryn groaned, shaking her head as I smiled at the thought of our baby girl being *anything* like me.

In some ways, for sure. But I already knew her finest traits would be inherited from her dope ass mama whose belly I started to rub when I said, "Almost can't believe she'll be here tomorrow."

"Shit's terrifying," Camryn sighed, my eyebrow raising as I asked, "You're scared?"

"Hell yeah, I'm scared," she whined before questioning, "You're not?"

If she would've asked me before my talk with her father, I would've been right there with her. But the truth was, "Nah, not anymore. I know I got what it takes to be a good father, and I know you got what it takes to bring her into the world safely. You're one of the toughest people I know, Camryn. Everything will be fine."

"Yeah, alright. Keep that same energy tomorrow when I'm cussing your ass out in-between contractions," she insisted as she maneuvered back under the covers and I followed, tossing my arm around her belly to spoon her when I replied, "You can cuss me out all you want to. I'll still be right there no matter what."

While the advice Mr. Teddy had given me had been directed towards parenting, I knew the same could be applied to how I approached supporting Camryn during tomorrow's delivery as well. But even with that mindset, it was still wild to think that in less than twenty-four hours, our worlds would be changed forever.

––––––––––

Shit was getting real.

We'd been up since the crack of dawn making sure we had everything we needed for the labor and after delivery, triple-checking the hospital bag and the nursery to ensure everything was in place for when we brought the baby home. And now that it was actually time for Camryn's labor to be induced, the countdown was on until I got to lay eyes on my baby girl, the excitement of it all setting me up for what ended up being a long ass day.

In my head, I assumed they'd give Camryn the drug to jumpstart her contractions, and then baby Keily would be out shortly after. But nah, that wasn't the case at all, the drug only the beginning of what ended up being a damn lesson in labor since this shit was nothing like what we'd learned about in class or what I'd seen in movies.

When Camryn's contractions finally started to kick up, they had to manually break her water, only making the contractions even more intense until they administered an epidural. And from there, Camryn was mostly chillin' as she continued to dilate - *slowly* - a nurse checking in on us intermittently as we spent the afternoon doing regular shit.

Watching TV and eating lunch.

Spending some time with family until Camryn started kicking everybody out for getting on her nerves.

Dishing out endless back massages and forehead kisses.

But naturally, as the day progressed, Camryn started getting restless, the epidural helping with the pain but not exactly doing anything for her mental even though the nurse told us not to worry. And Dr. Strong pretty much echoed the sentiment with claims that we just had a "stubborn one" on our hands.

"Just like her mama," I joked, Camryn rolling her eyes at me before closing them to get some rest. And as I watched her sleep, I couldn't get over how grateful I was that she was even putting her body through all of this for me - *for us* - more than ready to show my appreciation in every way possible as I snuck a little nap in myself before being woken up by Dr. Strong's announcement.

"Looks like you might be ready to push, Camryn."

Oh shit.

Getting in position next to the bed, I started using all the tactics I'd learned in class.

Encouraging deep breaths.

Giving eye contact between pushes as support.

Letting her break my fuckin' hand if she needed to.

Staying calm even though I was anxious as fuck.

Still, no matter how much she pushed, the baby wasn't making enough progress. And after catching the startled look on Dr. Strong's face when she peeked up at the monitors and then over to the nurse, I started growing nervous;

though the nurse remained completely calm when she suggested, "How about we take a break?"

"Why? What's wrong? Is something wrong?" Camryn asked, literally shaking as she worked to catch her breath.

Moving to the opposite side of the bed, Dr. Strong answered, "You're giving great pushes, Camryn. But as I'm watching the heart rate monitor, I'm worried we're putting the baby under a little too much distress right now. Let's try again in about an hour, okay?"

Because she didn't want to put the baby in any danger, Camryn gave a trembling nod that forced me to ask, "Hey, Doc. Why is she shaking so much?"

"They're called labor shakes. It's a mix of hormones, adrenaline, and temperature changes, and it's totally normal. Just give her a warm blanket and some love, and she should be fine."

Nodding, I followed her instructions to a tee, refusing to leave Camryn's side during the hour break that felt like a day in itself. And even though she wasn't saying much, I could tell by the look in her eyes that she was grateful I was there, the two of us just staring at each other when Dr. Strong returned to say, "Camryn, we're gonna give it another go. But please be aware, if things don't work out this time, we may have to go the C-section route."

While I knew Camryn was down to do whatever it took to deliver the baby safely, the determined look on her face told me she wasn't here for the alternative which meant this was it. And honestly, I almost started shaking with adrenaline myself when I told her, "You got this, mamas. I love you so much."

"I love you too, but I hate you right now," she groaned, making me laugh as I advised, "Push like you're taking it out on me then."

It was easy for her to agree to that as Dr. Strong said, "Alright, Camryn. Give it everything you got on three," before issuing a countdown that had Camryn clenching and grunting until she was out of breath.

"Let's give her some oxygen for the next one," Dr. Strong said, the nurse quickly covering Camryn's face with a mask before giving another countdown.

"And one, two..."

On three, I felt my hand crack and was tempted to scream right along with my girl since that shit hurt like hell. But knowing it was nothing compared to what she was currently enduring, I was forced to chill as Dr. Strong cheered, "Yes, that was perfect, Camryn. One more good one and we'll have the head."

The mention of the head had me taking a quick peek down below that I wished I wouldn't have once I saw what was going on.

Is that all Keily's hair?

And is that... shit?

Once I saw the pan being replaced, I realized it was definitely shit. But considering how hard Camryn was pushing and the fact that she really didn't have all that much control of her lower half thanks to the epidural, it made sense, a strained smile on my face as I swallowed hard and coached, "Come on, mamas. One more. Tuck that chin wit' it."

Camryn gave an enthusiastic nod like I'd told her exactly what she needed to hear to give the final push that allowed Dr. Strong to announce, "Congratulations, parents. Meet your baby girl."

Quickly placing her near Camryn's chest to hold while they wiped her clean, the both of us started crying as we looked at her for the first time, that love at first sight shit Mr. Teddy had talked about beyond valid as Camryn wailed,

"Oh my God, she's so perfectttt. Maverick, look at our daughter."

I couldn't take my eyes off of her if I wanted to, tears streaming down my face as Dr. Strong said, "Dad, we need you to cut the umbilical cord for us."

With shaky hands, I accepted the scissors and managed to get the job done, a permanent smile on my face as I studied the baby's features while Dr. Strong informed us, "Camryn, we need you to deliver the placenta and then we're looking at a first-degree tear we'll need to stitch up. While we're doing that, they're going to check her out really quick to make sure everything looks good, and then she'll be all yours."

Since the baby was being moved over to the medical station to get evaluated, I was too; though I didn't leave Camryn's side without telling her, "Finish strong, mamas. I'll watch Keily."

That made her smile as I peeked in on baby girl who was wiggling about, giving just the slightest cry when the nurse started suctioning her nose.

It was beautiful.

Literally everything about her was perfection.

And I couldn't have been more excited when the nurse told me, "Dad, we'll have you go ahead and place the baby onto Camryn's chest for the sacred hour. And then whenever you're ready, you can invite your family back to meet the new addition."

Once she was in my hands, I didn't want to let her go. But because I knew how important that first hour of skin-to-skin was for the two of them, I followed directions, gently placing Keily onto Camryn who looked every bit of exhausted yet excited as she stared down at our creation.

At God's creation.

Really, all of this had been orchestrated by Him one way or another.

Yeah, the pregnancy might've been unplanned, an accident, an "oops" if you will. But as I stared down at the two I loved most, it was clear now more than ever that everything had always been by design.

EPILOGUE

One year later.

Camryn

I almost couldn't believe that a year had already passed. But as I looked down at my daughter who'd decided she was going to celebrate her first birthday with a casual stroll across the room instead of staying the tiny, crawling baby I felt like I'd just given birth to, I found myself teary-eyed as I reflected on everything that had happened since she'd joined our world.

Her first Christmas.

Celebrating her father's twenty-sixth birthday.

Her first movie role thanks to GiGi Meredith.

Celebrating my twenty-seventh birthday.

Her first international vacation to Cabo San Lucas thanks to Maverick's generous donation the night she was conceived.

And now we were celebrating her first birthday, her father going all out in a way only he could like Keily would even remember any of it. But over time, I'd learned this was just one of the many ways he showed love; a language I'd grown to appreciate, especially since I'd been the benefactor on more than a few occasions.

That was the other amazing part of the past year.

While Maverick and I had fallen deeply in love with each other over the course of my pregnancy, meeting Maverick the dad only made that feeling grow ten-fold. He was so good with Keily, so loving and attentive. And honestly, for as much as I'd doubted him early on before the baby was even a thing, I realized now that I couldn't have picked a better person to have a child with, his relationship with our daughter so reminiscent of the one I had with my own father that it literally brought tears to my eyes watching the two of them jack around.

Well... maybe that wasn't the only reason I was crying. But for now, I was blaming it on that, interrupting the two of them to ask, "Can Mommy get some love too?"

"Any time she wants," Maverick answered, kissing my cheek before he scooped up the little girl who was practically his twin. But the fact that she looked just like him only made me love her even more, so enamored with our little family as she extended her arms to me for a quick hug and then did the true daddy's girl thing by immediately returning to her father.

They made me sick.

Still, I was so grateful for the both of them, unable to stop smiling as Maverick said, "Keily Girl, let's show Mommy what's in your pocket."

The fact that they even put real pockets on some baby clothes was hilarious to me since it wasn't like there was anything they needed to carry. But when I saw what Maverick had Keily trying to pull out of hers, I damn near passed out, my eyes wide when I stepped back and breathily asked, "Mav, what the hell is that?"

Right on cue, all of our friends and family attending the birthday party started to gather around, clearly in on the whole thing as Maverick held an oblivious Keily tightly against his hip and answered, "Exactly what it looks like, mamas." Then he made his way down to one knee, holding our baby girl in one arm and the sparkling diamond ring she'd been carrying for who knows how long out in front of him to ask, "Camryn Cox, will you marry me?"

Considering I'd been on the verge of tears all day, this was just the thing to make the waterworks really fly as I proudly nodded my head yes, Maverick leaving Keily on the ground so that he could stand up and lift me in a hug. And with excited cheers happening all around us, it felt like I was in some sort of fairytale as we spent the rest of the night celebrating both our daughter's birthday and our engagement.

It was a perfect day spent with all of my favorite people, a day I'd truly never forget. And later that night, I knew Maverick wouldn't be able to forget it either once I handed him the pregnancy test I'd taken after our trip to Mexico with a one-word explanation.

"Oops."

The End

EXTRAS

Enjoyed this book?
Please leave a review on Amazon or Goodreads!

To stay up-to-date with all of Alexandra Warren's
happenings including samples and excerpts, visit
actuallyitsalexandra.com, like her Facebook page, or sign-up
for her newsletter!

Also, be sure to check out the *Oops!* playlist on Spotify and
Apple Music!

ALSO BY ALEXANDRA WARREN

Baggage Claimed
One Last Shot (Nymphs & Trojans Book 2) – Series
collaboration with Nicole Falls
Love Unsolicited
Uncovered Truths: A Novella